FOREW(

Very occasionally amongst all
published each year comes a ra
sweeps the reader into a thrilling
all the ingredients to sate the imagination of today's
youngsters, whilst interspersed with an innovative and
forward-thinking range of ideas and possibilities for the future.

"Tomorrow's Children" is such a find. Shining like a beacon
in the dark, it is not only steeped in suspense and mystery with
its combination of Sci-fi, Harry Potter type wizardry, and
Bond-styled escapism - to name a few of the ingredients - but
subtly interwoven within its context lies the promise of hope
for the Universe.

Set in 25th Century Spain, this exciting fantasy is a tale with a
difference as it follows the journey of a young boy setting out
to find his destiny. As he battles his way through to a
surprising and thrilling climax with a few good companions to
help him on his way, he overcomes a diversity of dangers and
dilemmas; faces evil characters and fearsome creatures; and
develops some amazing powers from the influences which
begin to surround him.

Though written with tomorrow's generation in mind, the
youngsters of today, many adults will find this vividly told tale
an exciting and intriguing read; its interlacing themes
challenging them to think positively about the future of
mankind.

For its sheer enjoyment and underlying message, this is a book
which, together with its hero, will live on in the reader's mind.

ISBN: 978-1-907407-02-4

THE BLACK LEAF PUBLISHING GROUP
83 Clipstone Rd West
Forest Town, Mansfield
NG190ED
Nottinghamshire
England

www.blackleafpublishing.com

Tomorrow 's Children

The first Volume of the Trilogy

"Legends of the Ells"

by

J.T. Wheeling

"I see Four Women :

One will bring you pain and strife,
One will call from mountains far,
One will seek to join your life,
One will be your guiding star."

DEDICATION

To my wonderful wife and our splendid family.

ACKNOWLEDGEMENTS

To my daughter Ginny for her valuable input, to my son-in-law Andrew for his I T help, to all my grandsons who read the tale and asked for more, to Sean Sevestre for his artwork and to the ladies of Cornerstones for their invaluable guidance.

CHAPTER ONE

1

Polonia, central Spain. Late February, 2436

Yani raced through the village, terror in his heart. The stamp of pursuing feet spurred him on. "Faster, faster!" he urged himself.

A glance behind showed Marc, whip in hand and anticipation stamped on his spotty face, almost within reach. The last beating had left Yani in agony for days. As he raced on, the hill to the cottage and safety seemed endless.

Marc's heavy steps came closer, then the dreaded "woosh" of his whip whistled through the air. Yani hunched his shoulders as it grazed past his back.

"Ha, get you next time," gloated the voice behind.

At that moment Yani saw Senga the Healer's house. In desperation he veered right, flinging himself against Senga's door. Sobbing for breath he collapsed, banging his shoulder as he fell. The door opened and a tall gaunt woman stepped out calmly, as if she had been expecting him. Her leathery hands gripped a long cane which she pointed straight at Marc, who jerked to a stop.

"What do you think you're doing?" she barked.

Marc stepped back, "We were just playing," he whined, "and this—"

Senga prodded him. "Nonsense, you were going to beat him up again, you monster. Last time I had to dress his wounds and he couldn't work for a week. Your father was not pleased!"

"Old witch!" Marc muttered under his breath as he backed away, "When I run the village I'll see you burn!"

Senga's eyes blazed, "And who will tend the sick after me? Get off home or I'll speak to your father, then we'll see how you enjoy a thrashing."

Marc remembered only too well the strength of his father's arm and his uncertain temper. Sullenly he turned and lumbered off down the hill.

Senga helped Yani to his feet and smiled. The boy's hair gleamed golden in the evening sun, his blue eyes huge in the slim face. Despite his ordeal, he looked defiant.

"Thank you, Senga," he said. "I must run faster 'till I'm big enough to fight him. I'll be fourteen next week."

"He's a stupid bully who doesn't know any better, and his sister's worse." Yani's face tightened as he remembered black- haired Lula and her cruel eyes.

"I must get back to Mika, he hasn't been eating."

"Why don't you just run off from this miserable place?"

"Mika cared for me when I was small. Now he needs me."

Senga shrugged and shook her head. "Well, here's some beef broth, that'll give him strength, and a bone for that dog of yours. I'll watch while you go up the hill."

Mika lay half awake, thoughts flickering like a dying candle. He imagined it must be evening; if so, Yani would be back soon. Yani, golden haired Yani. At the thought of the faithful boy who had cared for him since he had come back to this god-forsaken village—what was it?—seven years ago, a smile touched his shrunken, bristled face. Yani's fine features, filled by the remarkable sapphire eyes, swam before him. Mika blinked and realized that the boy had actually come in. He could stop dreaming, Yani had returned. Bob, released from his chain, padded around the room carrying a bone.

"Yani," he whispered as, muscles protesting, he tried to sit up.

- "Look," Yani said, "Senga's sent you some broth. Let me help you up."

"Listen Yani," Mika wheezed, gathering his wits to speak, "This winter's done for me and I've been thinking about your future. You must get away from here and go and find your white city in the south. When I die, Jord will seize this cottage and make you live in his stables." At the sound of Jord's name Bob looked up and growled softly.

2

Yani swallowed. "But you're not going to die. I'm here and—."

"No, boy, my end is coming. I feel it. I have walked in too many winds. Don't argue, just listen. Your birthday's in a week and Senga told me that Jord will be away with his men that day. Leave early in the morning and get to the forest that lies in the south. I managed to hide a little money from Jord, you'll find it under the hearthstone there."

Yani blinked hard to hide his tears.

"You've been a true friend to me, Yani. I'm sorry I ever brought you to this place—"

"But you had no idea what had happened to it since you left."

"Just you remember what I've said. Now I'm going to sleep and you make your plans. Spring is coming, that'll help. Goodnight my boy! Play your mouth organ for me, it helps me settle." Mika turned away and closed his eyes, putting an end to any further discussion.

Yani unwrapped his precious mouth organ and went outside. The little three roomed cottage huddled comfortably against the hillside, with the village lights twinkling below. Above, stars sprinkled the spring sky. Yani sat down on a log and played one gypsy song after another until Mika fell asleep. Only then did the boy go to bed.

That night when Yani was sleeping a gentle presence entered his dreams and counselled him, as it had done every night since he could remember.

"Soon, Yani, you will be fourteen and your powers will begin to waken. Till then you must be patient."

Yani rose early and left before Mika woke. Jord inspected the stables every morning and there would be trouble if they weren't mucked out thoroughly. On the way down he saw a light in Senga's window. He knocked on her door.

"How did he like the broth?"

"It did him good, but now he's talking about dying and…"

"I'll go up and see him. You'd better get off now. Stop by on your way home and I'll tell you what I think."

Yani laboured hard and Jord left him in peace. Better still, he learned that Marc and Lula were away. At last, his work finished, Yani hurried back to Senga, anxious to hear her opinion.

Senga sighed, "I'm afraid he can't last much longer, Yani. Afterwards you must leave at once. Tomorrow you have the day off and I'm afraid you'll have to spend the time digging a grave behind the cottage. Mika would like to be buried there."

During the next six days Mika slept more and more and, while Yani worked, Senga spent her day sitting with her friend. Every night Yani hurried back, expecting the worst, but Mika hung on, as if waiting for Yani's birthday.

Just after midnight the old man's eyes opened and he smiled.

"Happy Birthday, Yani" he whispered, clasping his hand. Yani leant closer to catch each word, "Time to go our separate ways. Sorry I can't come with you," then Mika sighed softly and his eyes closed for the last time.

"No, Mika, come back," the boy cried then, realizing this was their final parting, buried his head on the familiar chest and sobbed his heart out. After some time he got up, dried his face and went down the hill to fetch Senga. That night they buried Mika where he had wished, in his own garden.

"You haven't time to grieve, Yani, leave now."

"I have today off," Yani said, "there are a few things I get each Sunday from the store. If I don't appear someone might be suspicious. Jord's group are away smuggling again, so I shall be well gone by the time they notice. But what about you, shouldn't you leave too?"

Senga snorted. "I've lived all my life here and most of the folk are decent enough, just scared of Jord and his gang. You go and seek the white city you remember. But you're right, keep to your usual routine. No one should miss you till Monday. I could send a message to Jord saying you're sick, that might give you more time."

"Senga, I'll never forget you!"

4

"On you go," mumbled the old woman, turning away. She couldn't recall the last time she had shed tears.

"Get a little sleep, boy. You'll need it and dawn's coming soon. Go with my blessing," and, to his surprise, Yani received a great hug before Senga turned and left.

Yani woke early. Leaving Bob locked in, he set off down to the village to do his weekly trade of rabbits for provisions. All was quiet as he jogged down the hill, the sun warm on his back and the spring flowers scenting the morning air. He took a deep breath. His duty to Mika was done and now he could escape this place. He hoped his tormentors were still away.

A stone whistled past his ear, bouncing off the wall beyond.

"Yah-nee, Yah-nee, dirty Ell, dirty Ell!" came the nauseating chant.

He whirled round, heart thumping. Lula, proud of her young body, stood beside Marc. Behind her stood her big cousin, Venty, piggy eyes gleaming in a pock-marked face. Lula pointed a broomhandle at Yani.

"Got you this time." Triumph shone in her black eyes. She had always hated him ever since that time....Yani's thoughts snapped back to the present.

"How nice! He's trapped some rabbits to welcome us back. Give 'em here!"

"No!" Yani backed away.

"Go on, Marc, get him before he runs. Let's strip him and throw him in the dung heap, that's where dirty Ells belong." Marc, a full head taller than Yani, reached out to grab Yani's hair.

Last night the dream message had changed. "Today is your fourteenth birthday, now your powers awaken and you can begin to fight."

Yani dropped the rabbits, caught Marc's hand, twisted it, spun round, and used the bigger lad's momentum to bash him against the wall. Feeling Vanity's hands on his shoulders he dropped into a ball, hooking his arms backwards and outside his attacker's legs. He tucked in his chin, heaved up and threw

5

Venty over, to fall on top of Marc and cracking their heads together.

He staggered to his feet, gaping at the two bullies lying dazed, wondering what had possessed him. A noise came from behind. Yani ducked and Lula's broom handle wooshed over his head. Before she could take a second swipe at him, he leapt forward and grabbed it.

Twisting and turning the handle, Yani began to break her hold. Lula gasped as she tried to tug it away. Where had all this strength come from? It had always been easy to bully him and make those dark eyes fill with tears.

She dropped the handle and stepped back. "You're a witch!" she gasped, "and witches should be burned, yes, burned alive!" She licked her fat lips. "Wait till I tell Jord how you witched extra strength and hurt his son. He'll see you burn."

Yani recoiled in horror—was he really a witch? Ever since Mika had brought him here from the gypsies the youngsters had resented him. His different appearance irritated them and he knew they would just as well get rid of him. But—a burning!

Heart pounding and still holding the handle, he picked up the rabbits and ran to the store. Quickly collecting what he needed, Yani then sprinted up the hill to the cottage.

He released Bob, who had been whining anxiously. The big dog jumped up and, putting his paws on Yani's shoulders, gave the boy a comforting lick. Yani hugged him back, knowing that with Bob beside him, he was safe. His tormentors hated the big hound for protecting him. He threw his few belongings into an old haversack, grabbed the broom handle as his only weapon, only to hesitate at the door.

This had been his home for seven years caring for Mika as the kindly old man grew weaker. Seven years—and they had only intended to stay a few days. Jord had put a stop to that. The horrible memory sprang up as if it had been yesterday.

"Now Yani," Mika had said as they neared Polonia, "I promised your gypsy friends to return you and Bob to the white city by the sea, the one you remember leaving when you were three."

"Nearly four," Yani corrected him. "I had my birthday as we travelled north. Now I'm seven."

"The thing is I need to stop here at my old village for a few days, to see if my cottage is still standing and make some arrangements."

An old stone building came into view, overgrown, dirty and deserted.

"Well, it's still there. We can leave the ponies in the field and walk down to the village," Mika said, then scratched his grey head. "I wonder who's running things now?"

By the following evening Mika was putting things back into his saddlebags.

"Are we leaving already, Mika?"

"I don't like what I see. That thug Jord has taken over control. This is not a place for you, so we shall leave tomorrow."

"Oh no, you won't!" growled a voice from the doorway. "Run off and report what we do here—I think not."

The hulking shape of Jord, self-appointed head of the village, filled the doorway. Bob's growl sounded from behind the kitchen door.

Yani sprang up in front of Mika. He glared at Jord who loomed over him, unkempt and smelling of beer and rank sweat.

Mika came across the room.

"You're not welcome in my house," he said. "You were a bully when you were a child and you're no better now. Just get out."

"Not till I've seen your money!"

Yani clenched his hands and stepped forward. Jord's great fist stunned the boy who collapsed on the floor, then he picked up Mika and shook him violently.

"Where is it?" he rasped.

"You'll get nothing from me and tomorrow I'll be gone from this forsaken place."

"It's my village now and you're going nowhere!" Dropping Mika, Jord picked up an iron poker, swung it twice and smashed the old man's ankles. Mika screamed and tried to drag himself away. Bob barked furiously from the kitchen and scrabbled at the door.

"Your money," Jord repeated, "or shall I start on the boy?"

"Take it!" Mika gasped, "it's in my saddlebag."

Jord grinned and helped himself as Yani tried to get up. Jord turned and planted his dirty boot on the boy's chest.

"Like I said, you're going nowhere—ever again. You can work for me, cleaning the stables and cowsheds. I'll take the ponies in case you're tempted to try and run."

Ferocious growls and scratches continued from the kitchen door. Jord gave it a nervous glance, then added, "Another thing, keep that large dog up here or you'll find it poisoned, that's a promise." He turned on his heel and left.

Dizzy and sick, Yani crawled over to Mika. Barely conscious, sweat beading his brow, the old man forced his eyes open. Slowly they focussed on Yani's crumpled face. His voice rasped.

"Yani, boy, listen. Go and get Senga. First house on the left near the foot of the hill. Tell her about this. She'll sort out my legs. Afterwards, you get away. Go south and take Bob."

White-faced and sick, Yani made his promise, "I'll get Senga but I'm not leaving you. You've cared for me, now it's my turn."

Mika's eyes closed again as the pain took him; he couldn't get any more words out, and Yani went off to find Senga.

Now, after seven years, he could leave with a clear conscience. He could do no more for Mika. "Come on Bob," he murmured, "we're on the road at last." He chose the track going south, along the bare, rocky hillside and prayed they would not bother to come after him.

The light was fading before sounds of pursuit alarmed him. Somewhere ahead lay a forest where he could hide. He started to run but the ominous pounding of hoofs on the hard ground grew louder. His legs spasmed and his lungs were on fire; he

8

could go no faster. A line of trees appeared in the distance but it would take too long to reach them.

"There he is! We've got him!" Jord's triumphant shout made Yani turn. His heart fell then, suddenly, fury flared in his head. He stopped running and turned to face the six men galloping towards him over the stony ground.

Bob, hackles up, jumped in front of him, and bared his teeth. The group pulled up a stone's throw away. "Leave me alone," Yani shouted. "Go back!"

Jord's harsh voice mocked him. "Listen to the little squirt. Go back, he says. I wonder what he'll say when we roast him? Lula says he's a witch." Lowering his hunting spear he rode straight at Bob.

Without thinking, Yani jumped forward, pointing his broom handle at Jord. "No!" he yelled.

Crack! A fiery bolt struck Jord full in the chest, catapulting him out of his saddle onto the ground. The other riders recoiled in surprise. Yani, as amazed as everyone else, heard his own voice, shrill with fear. "Push off, or I'll burn you all. Leave the pony. Go!"

Venty and Marc spurred their ponies forward. The handle in Yani's hand seemed to crackle with power, then spat more flashes. Venty and Marc joined Jord, all lying senseless on the ground.

The remaining three backed off, utterly astonished. Whatever had happened to the Yani that had obeyed them? Truly this was an entirely different creature. Lula had been right, he must be a witch, but also very dangerous and best left alone.

Not trusting himself to move, Yani stood still, legs shaking, and watched the three disappear back along the track. His knees finally gave way and he sank to the ground. What had possessed him? How had he done what he had done—or was it the handle? Bob's wet nose in his face roused him from his thoughts. Still shaking, he scrambled to his feet.

"Oh Bob," he said, stroking the thick coat, "you wouldn't have let them take me would you? Now we'd better get on in case they change their mind."

Ignoring the three moaning bodies on the ground, Yani used the rope they had brought to bind him to tether two ponies behind Hardy, the one he knew best.

"Now we can really travel, Bob," he said, as he clattered into the forest.

Late that night Yani reached a small town and sold the two ponies for some much needed money.

"That'll make up for some of what Jord stole from Mika," he mused as he entered the local inn. There he was accepted; custom this early in the year was welcome, even from a ragged youngster.

Next day, with only a distant memory of a white city by a warm sea to guide him, Yani followed the road through the forest, travelling towards the sun. Years with the gypsies had taught him how to live off the land. He also had other skills that he didn't fully understand, for every morning he seemed to have learned something in his dreams. The lady who spoke to him as he slept never showed her face, but her voice was gentle and loving.

"Who is she, Bob?" he asked. "I have the feeling that I knew her long ago, but you've always been with me too. Did you know her, does she visit your dreams too?"

Bob, trotting alongside, lifted his old shaggy head and looked at his master with adoration. As they travelled, Yani kept his sling to hand. Years of practice had made him accurate at bringing down the odd meal, rabbit or bird, so they wouldn't starve.

Solitude was fine, he had Bob and now he had Hardy, the best of the village ponies. At last he was free, and would come to somewhere eventually. But how had he won his freedom? He eyed his staff (as he called the broom handle) with suspicion. He had tried to get it to shoot bolts again, but nothing happened. Perhaps it was bewitched, or perhaps he

10

was a—No! he couldn`t be....his thoughts shied away from such an idea .

Finding a suitable spot to camp near a small stream, Yani tethered his pony and chose some food from his pack. Suddenly Bob jumped up, staring into the trees and growling deep in his throat.

"What do you hear, boy?" he whispered. It was then he heard the low, throaty growl of another animal, and saw something large and black slink out of the undergrowth. The female lynx weaved in front of him, her paws silent on the mossy ground. Bob snarled at her and before Yani could pull him to heel, he had moved out of reach. Yellow eyes shone in the lynx`s dark face, her whiskers quivering as she bared her teeth and hissed at the hound. "Stay back, Bob," Yani commanded, panic rising at every word. He looked around for his handle but found it too late.

The animals rose in unison to collide in mid air, Bob with a death grip at her throat as they fell to the ground with a sickening thud. Yani could do nothing but stand and watch as the animals writhed and ripped at each other. He sought an opening to strike the lynx with his staff, but he was afraid he would hit his dog instead. The hound's powerful jaws were clamped over the lynx.s windpipe, Yani could see the animal was gasping for breath, her flailing claws beginning to ebb. Bob wrestled her to the ground, growling into her bloody throat. She struggled futilely, terrible sounds escaping her snapping jaws, till eventually she lay still and quiet, her chest unmoving. "Leave it Bob," Yani ordered, approaching slowly, afraid the animal would somehow regain consciousness. He had never been this close to something so magnificent and so dangerous. The hound extricated his muzzle from the cat and sank to his side whining, his front paws lifted away from his wounded under-belly.

Yani poked the cat to be sure it was dead before turning his attention to his dog, and only then did he see the damage that had been inflicted. He sank to his knees, and tried in vain to

11

close the gaping wounds. Ripping his shirt to pieces he tried to stop the flowing blood with makeshift bandages.

"Stupid, stupid dog," he scolded through his tears, "I told you to stay back, I could have dealt with it, why didn't you obey me?" He lifted his faithful friend's head on to his lap to hold him close. "Don't leave me Bob," he sobbed, "don't leave me all alone. We have been through worse than this, you and me, much worse, you're going to be okay."

Bob gave a great sigh. His head sank slowly into Yani's lap and his body became heavy and still. Yani sat, rocking his pet, his comrade-in-arms, backwards and forwards. Grief, and a numbing sense of aloneness, held him in a timeless grip.

The first rays of the sun woke Yani. Missing the familiar cold nose nuzzling his ear, he suddenly recalled the fight. For a time he lay unmoving, a black aching hole in his heart. He could not remember a time when Bob had not been with him. Ever since that distant day, when he had come back from exploring the woods with the gypsy boy to find his parents' caravan buried under a rockfall, Bob had protected him. All the three years with the gypsy clan, all the seven years in Polonia, Bob had been his constant companion.

Now he was gone, giving his life to protect him. No other animal had so loved him: it had been a life of total devotion. He could never make it up to Bob now.

"But I'll make you proud of me, Bob," he swore between sobs, "I will be as brave as you've been and as loyal to my friends—if I ever find any," he added wistfully.

Eventually he roused himself and scraped a shallow grave with his knife before building a cairn over it with the biggest stones he could move. Now Bob's body would be safe from scavengers.

"Everything I love leaves me, Bob. First my parents, then Mika, now you."

He tried to say "Goodbye" but his voice failed him. At last he turned away and, with an empty heart, took the road south without looking back.

Travelling

Two days later Yani came to the end of the forest. Far ahead, across a bare plain, he saw a long line of hills.

"There'll be no cover for us to hide up there, Hardy," he said, glancing back nervously from time to time for any sign of pursuit. "Do you think they might try again?"

Towards evening he started to look for a place to sleep. The lynx's attack had put him off camping and last night he had managed to talk an innkeeper into giving him cheap accommodation.

"It's a challenge my father has set me," he had said. "He's teaching me to manage money so he's given me a little and I've to travel to Cordoba by myself and make it last. How much is your cheapest bed?"

The landlord had smiled and said, "Well, if you really want to save money, you can have the room off the stables for free," and Yani had gladly accepted.

Now, a day later, the light was fading again but he could see lights twinkling in the distance.

"Come on Hardy," he urged his pony, digging in his heels, "you're as hungry as I am." Thus encouraged, Hardy snorted and quickened his pace.

The main village street was deserted but a sign "Torreperogil Inn" hung on a long three-storey building. Yani tethered Hardy to a post and went inside. The big gloomy hall smelt of lavender and polish, but no one seemed to be about.

"Hola!" Yani called tentatively.

"Can I help you?" boomed a deep voice, startling him. Yani spun round to see a tall woman advancing on him, like a galleon under sail. He swallowed nervously, then launched into his story. Halfway through, he saw the disbelief in her eyes

"Humph!" she said. "Where's your pony?"

"Tethered outside."

For a moment she inspected him in silence from a pair of dark eyes. "Pinto!" she called in a voice like a foghorn. Yani edged towards the entrance, but she forestalled him by moving swiftly to the door and closing it.

Pinto appeared, an ancient gnome of a man, half the height of his employer, and smaller than Yani. "Yes, ma`am?"

"Fetch in this young lad`s saddle bags, then take the pony to Manuel`s stable and hide it there. If anyone asks, you`ve never seen this boy before."

Seeing the alarm rising in Yani`s face, the woman suddenly smiled, producing a line of large teeth. "It`s for your own protection, lad," she rumbled.

"Protection?"

"I am the Widow Grimstone," she announced, "I`ve heard about you but don`t worry, you`ll be safe here."

"You`ve heard about me?"

She flashed the tombstones at him again, and Yani began to wonder what had happened to Mr. Grimstone.

"You must be starving, lad. Come to the kitchen and we`ll see what we can find."

As long as I`m not on the menu, Yani thought, then, curiosity overcoming him, asked again, "You`ve heard about me?" as he followed her down a dark corridor.

"We may live in the wilds, but we do have communications you know."

In fact, Yani did not know and had never heard of `communications`.

"Satellite V-phones," she explained, which didn`t help either. "My cousin owns the inn where you stayed last night. He called me earlier and said that a bunch of ruffians had just left. They had been asking for you and seemed to think you were on the Cordoba road."

"I must go!" Yani gasped, turning round.

"No lad, I told you, you are perfectly safe here," she said, putting a large hand on his shoulder. "You need food, rest, and then some help. I`ll take care of anyone chasing you, never fear, but you`d better tell me your story, the real one I mean."

14

They reached the kitchen, a warm comfortable room with hams and cheeses hanging from the rafters.

"First you must eat, then you can decide whether or not to trust me," the Widow said in a kindly tone. Having placed large quantities of food on the table, she sat down and watched the famished boy attack it. Despite his unkempt appearance, he spoke well and had reasonable manners. She noted the slim hands, the fine-drawn features, the intelligent eyes; this was no rascal.

As he ate, Yani decided to trust this strange woman; there had been no need for her to tell him that she knew he was being hunted. He felt surprise, Jord must be keen to get him back—or to silence him. He looked up at her, smiled and told her all he could remember since the avalanche ten years ago.

After listening carefully, she sat deep in thought. Finally she spoke.

"This is a shocking thing, Yani. Would you like me to arrange for you to be accompanied on your journey. I could speak to the town guard and—"

"Oh no! Thank you, but no! I must make my own way," Yani replied quickly, unsure about involving officials in his life. Something of the gypsies' independence and even the villagers' hatred of authority had become second nature to him.

The Widow Grimstone saw the determination in his eyes. She also saw wariness. Well, she would do what she could for him. From a tall cabinet she selected a long scroll of paper, which she unrolled on the table.

"This is a map," she rumbled. "Look, we are here," pointing to a small circle where several roads met.

"Your hunters will be about there," placing a boney finger further east and north. "They will expect you to go southwest towards Linares and Cordoba. Instead, follow this route southeast through the mountains and down to the Cuavas de Agua. After that you can work your way south and west, to Guadix, Granada and then down to the sea. Your white city must lie somewhere along that coast. But are you sure you don't want to be escorted? The guards are good people."

"No thank you," Yani said again. "I can't explain it but I must do this on my own." The Widow shrugged her shoulders. "First you need to get a good rest," she said firmly.

"Pinto," she called down the corridor, "are the bags in the boy's room, and did you settle the pony?"

"All done," came the reply .

"Right, I will lock up. We have no guests and no one else is to be admitted for any reason. You go to bed now. Goodnight!"

The Widow smiled and patted Yani's shoulder as she showed him into his room. "Sleep well, lad," she said. Tired and well fed, Yani tumbled into bed and fell fast asleep. Sometime in the middle of the night he woke, to hear a clatter of hooves followed by loud banging on the stout door.

"What do you think you are doing at this hour," boomed the Widow's voice from an upstairs window.

"We are trying to find a boy who stole some ponies. He was seen travelling towards here yesterday."

"A boy with golden hair on a brown pony?"

"That's him."

"Oh, I didn't like the look of him; I don't let ragamuffins in my place. I sent him on his way pretty smartly. He wanted to get to Seville and took the Cordoba road. Can I call the town guard to assist you? It'll be no trouble--"

"No, no, don't bother them, we'll manage on our own!" came a rapid reply, and the men turned and clattered off at speed.

The Widow came down to see if Yani had been woken by the noise. "Did you recognize any of those voices?" she asked.

Yani shook his head. "No, I didn't, so why should they be hunting me?"

"Perhaps your village friends are part of a wider group and sent out messages to their colleagues. Anyway, they've gone and you can sleep till morning. I've looked out some better clothes for you. They belonged to my son and should fit you well enough." She dropped a bundle on a chair as she left.

At breakfast, the widow produced a large sack of provisions and a map. "This is the way you should go. It`s seldom used so you`re unlikely to meet anyone. Around Guadix you`ll find many habitations tunnelled into the rock. In the olden days that was how people escaped the summer heat, but the place is deserted now. You could sleep there if you wish." She repressed another impulse to suggest the guards help him, deterred by the resolve in his young face.

"Good luck, Yani, and let me know when you find your city," she called after him as he left. She watched till he had disappeared, then turned and called the town guard in Cordoba. Someone should discourage the band of ruffians from hunting the boy.

As he rode along the dusty track, Yani wondered if he had been foolish to refuse the Widow`s offer of help. Deep inside, he felt that his journey, long or short, would help him discover his capabilities. Up to now his life had been controlled by others, now he would make his own way.

After three hours steady riding the high ridge the Widow had mentioned appeared on the horizon. "You will see a hill to the right of the road with strange looking boulders at the top. Travellers speak of a magnetic pull tempting them to climb up and explore. You`re a brave lad but I suggest you pass it by. Curiosity is as dangerous for people as it is for cats!"

The noonday sun bounced off the barren ground and Yani was both hungry and thirsty by the time he reached the saddle that cut through the ridge. Dismounting by a group of trees, he opened the sack of provisions the Widow had given him.

While he ate, he found his eyes being drawn to the boulders crowning the hill above. From where he sat they had the appearance of tall figures; he decided a closer look would be interesting. He left Hardy tethered in the shade and started to climb.

The nearer he got, the greater the resemblance the rocks had to tall people. An air of great peace and tranquillity hung

17

round the place, but Yani sensed also an aura of regret and farewell. He had the impression that something great and noble had passed this way and gone beyond to some other realm, never to return. Only the wind remained, lamenting around the stones; there was nothing else. The boy stopped a short distance from the rocks, torn between a desire to touch them and a strong sense that he should not. As in his dreams a voice seemed to speak in his head.

"Someday you too will pass this way, but that is not yet. Follow your destiny for there is much for you to do. Leave your fears behind; in the end, all will be well."

A feeling of comfort settled around him, yet tears filled his eyes. "Yes," he whispered, "yes, I will go and find my destiny. I am here for some purpose, though what it may be I do not yet know."

Reluctantly he turned and made his way back down to where his pony waited. "Come, Hardy," he said, "we have far to go." Remounting, he rode forward with a new determination.

The bare hillside stretched down to a plain, sparsely studded with bushes. Towards evening the ground started to fall again and trees and grass softened the land. The skies darkened and there was a mutter of thunder in the hills behind.

To his surprise Yani heard the sound of a guitar and he caught a glimpse of caravans and horses among a stand of trees. His heart quickened, gypsies! Memories flooded back and he turned Hardy to investigate.

A group of about twenty were gathered round a fire, over which a pot hung, emitting wonderful smells. A tall weather-beaten man stood up as Yani approached. He did not look welcoming.

"Hola!" Yani called. "Have you any news of the Sandor family?"

"Sandor family? How do you know of the Sandor family?"

"They cared for me for years when I was small and my parents had been killed."

18

The tall man`s expression softened a little. "Yes," he said, "old Georgio told me of a boy with yellow hair they rescued— but that was long ago. He wanted to find his home and joined a traveller who promised to take him to the south coast."

"That was seven years ago and I`m still trying to get there."

"So you are that boy! Got lost, did you? Well, don`t sit up there talking, come down and join us, we`ve plenty of food. "

The years fell away and Yani found himself the centre of attention. Strangers were sources of news and with his old gypsy connection he aroused their curiosity. Bit by bit they pulled his story from him. Angry mutterings rose as Yani told of his time in Polonia and of Jord`s cruelty to Mica.

"But today I came over the road from Torreperogil and saw some curious rocks on a hilltop. They looked like people from below and—"

"I hope you kept well away, boy, that place is strange. Many of the great ones went there some time back and never returned. We call it the Hill of Farewell."

Yani frowned, "Great ones?" he asked.

"Yes, those who ruled the world for ages. We gypsies had little to do with them, but the old tales tell that they brought peace to a troubled world long ago."

"I could have done with their help," Yani thought to himself. "It`s a pity they`ve gone."

The old grandmother, whose walnut-like face suggested she had seen too many years to be surprised by anything, waved to him. "Sit by me, boy, and give me your hand."

She took it in her own wizened claw and studied it carefully. "Four women," she murmured, "in a long life. One will bring you pain and strife, one will call from mountains far, one will seek to share your life, one will be your guiding star."

Her old, rheumy eyes peered into Yani`s face and she laid her other hand on his head. "Remember you are as an arrow flying through time, guided by your thoughts. Trim them well, for you have far to go. Now, go and eat."

19

The threatened storm passed and, after the meal, Yani produced his mouth organ and joined the fiddles and guitars. Girls got up and danced around the fire, their shadows leaping on the painted caravans. Far above, a vast canopy of stars jewelled the velvet sky.

Yani played, danced, clapped and sang till he collapsed exhausted. He hadn"t had such fun in years. Perhaps, he thought drowsily as he lay wrapped in his blanket, this was the life for him, but again the voice came to him as he slept: "Yani, you are not a gypsy. They have helped you and given you their music but you must go on and find your own kind."

CHAPTER TWO

1

New Friends

"I like this simple life, travelling by caravan as the gypsies do," Lucy remarked to Pasco, her brother, as she tossed her brown hair back.

"Especially when we've got this big fellow to look after us," Pasco added, looking at the substantial figure of Turias, his American cousin, who was holding the reins lightly and keeping his eyes on the road ahead.

Turias shrugged his shoulders. "I know you're worried about that guy following us. I've been watching him for some time too."

"Well, we are meeting Zandor in Lahara because there's been some talk of outlaws" Lucy pointed out.

Her brother's dark eyes, so like her own, crinkled, "We'll protect you, little sister. Remember we've all been to the Tower."

At the word "little" Lucy thumped his arm. "You're not much bigger yourself. Our Ell blood isn't doing its stuff. We hardly grew at all at the Tower."

She looked behind. That figure following them on horseback, perhaps he was a real live outlaw; she clasped herself in excitement.

"Pasco, that fellow is still there. You said he would soon pass us…"

"Lucy, other travellers do use this road, and—"

"I think there's something strange about him."

"Can you two do something useful and have a look at the map." Turias'deep voice came from the front. "Somewhere there's a lake which could be a good place to stop."

Pasco opened the map and studied it. "There's a blue area about twenty kilometres ahead," he estimated, "that must be it."

Three hours later they reached the lake and made camp nearby. The sunset faded over the western hills and darkness closed around them.

Yani had found a sheltered spot off the track about three hundred metres behind them and settled down for the night. Wrapped in a blanket, he lay under the stars, thinking about the group he was following. They seemed happy youngsters, but he, a dirty Ell, would only alarm them if he got too close.

The sound of a number of horses moving quietly through the darkness alerted him. Still wary of pursuit, Yani and Hardy were well hidden among some bushes. Several men passed along the track, going stealthily. His suspicion aroused, Yani grabbed his broom handle and crept after them.

Around a campfire, the three youngsters watched their food cooking. "You're very good at this barbeque business, Turias," Lucy remarked.

"It's not difficult being better than Pasco, his burnt offering last night was—"

Without warning a group of mounted men loomed up out of the surrounding darkness and, before the youngsters could rise, cast heavy nets over them.

"Get this thing off me," Turias roared, trying to reach for his staff. "What do you think you're doing?"

"Taking valuable hostages," came the reply, "I suggest you—"

"We are Ells!" Pasco shouted. "Have you any idea of the punishment for this?"

"We know about you!" the voice mocked. "Young half Ells and not yet trained. Your time is passing and Lord Draach will be the new power here. You will be useful to him."

Lucy struggled with the netting...if she could just get her hands on her staff. She had been right about the man following them after all.

"Let's wrap'em up well lads, Draach will want them in good condition...especially the girl." He gave an unpleasant laugh.

Dismounting, all eight men came forward to secure the youngsters. Turias exerted his great strength to try to break free, but the net held.

A red bolt shot out of the dark, quickly followed by another and two men yelled and collapsed. Startled, the others turned to see where it had come from. Again there was a flash and a third man hit the ground. Leaving their captives, the remaining five leapt onto their horses.

Their leader shouted, "Out there, on the high ground," and the group thundered off up the hill.

"Lie still," said a voice in Turias's ear a minute later, and a knife started to saw at the netting. Turning his head, Turias saw a shock of bright hair framing a lean face, the eyes intent on the knife cutting the net.

"Who—?"

"Shush!" said the stranger, "They`ll be back any moment."

Soon all three had been cut loose. Quickly they tied the hands of the unconscious villains, then picked up their staffs.

"We should get out of the firelight" their rescuer suggested.

"Right," snapped Turias, longing to get his hands on the other men, "now we`ll surprise them."

A little later, hoofbeats sounded and the band returned.

"They`ve gone," a voice called in amazement. "Look, the nets are cut."

"Find them," the leader ordered, just before Lucy and Pasco`s staffs shot bolts and the leader and the man beside him were knocked off their horses. The last three of the group turned tail and bolted into the night.

"Wrap up these five in their own nets," the stranger suggested, "I shall go and chase the rest off properly. See you later." He jumped on one of the horses and disappeared into the night.

"But who are—?" Lucy called after him, but Pasco hurried her. "Quick, before these fellows recover. Help me wrap them in the netting."

Turias was already at work and it didn't take long to secure their prisoners. One man tried to resist but Turias's big fist silenced him.

Distant cracks sounded, suggesting their new friend was at work, but these faded to nothing and for a long time silence reigned.

"Do you think he's all right?" Lucy asked.

"He seemed pretty competent to me," Turias replied, "but who is he? I thought we were the last Ells around here."

The stars were paling before the stranger returned. He rode into the firelight and inspected the five captives with satisfaction.

"Do you want me to drop them in the lake?" he asked loudly, keeping a straight face. Furious but muffled protests showed that gags were in place.

The three youngsters looked up in surprise. "Can we discuss this away from their ears?" Turias suggested, and all four moved to the far side of the caravan. Pasco lit a lamp and Yani looked at them carefully. Turias, black haired and much taller than Yani, had a face like hewn teak. Pasco, almost Yani's height, sported the keen look of a hunting terrier, while Lucy's elfin face was alight with curiosity.

"First of all," said Turias, "How do we thank you for what you did? Please tell us where you come from and who you are? We thought all Ells had gone."

Yani's eyes flashed. "Who are you calling an Ell? Why insult me? I've just saved you from—."

Pasco gaped at him. "Insult you? We are all Ells and proud of it. Well, half-Ells anyway," he added. "I am Pasco, this is my sister Lucy and this great hulk is my cousin Turias, from America! What's your name?"

"Yani. What do you mean, you are all Ells? What are Ells anyway?"

The three gazed at him, utterly baffled.

"What are...come on, you must know. You used your staff to knock down these rascals."

24

"Not I," said Yani. "It's this old broomhandle. I think it's got some sort of magic inside."

Lucy slapped a hand over her mouth to stifle a giggle. This was a very serious, if confused, young lad—and not bad looking.

Turias spoke. "Listen Yani, apparently there is much you don't know. Why, I can't guess, but let me tell you that to be an Ell, or a half-Ell whose mother is Ell, is very special. Ells came from far away, hundreds of years ago, to sort out the mess this planet was in."

"Mess?"

"Well, wars, pollution, over-population…you name it, they had it."

"They, you mean us humans?"

"Yani, is that your full name? Yani, you must have at least one Ell parent or you couldn't shoot anger through that ..that broom thing."

Yani's eyes widened. "You mean it's me doing it?" He thought back. "Yes, only when I'm angry, it happens." Suddenly he remembered, "but then you did it too, both of you," looking at Lucy and Pasco.

"And to have Ell blood is a great blessing, but a curse too," Lucy put in.

Yani still seemed doubtful. Dubbed a "dirty Ell" for so long had degraded the word in his mind. He looked at Lucy. "Why a curse?" he asked.

"Because all pure Ells have left Earth, except for a few. They came a long time ago to save the planet and its people. Now humans must succeed or fail on their own. We who are half-Ell half-human can stay, but have already said farewell to our mothers."

Yani shook his head, bewildered by so many new concepts.

Turias suggested: "Join us on our journey, and we can talk as we go."

A great smile transformed Yani's face: companionship at last with people who seemed to know so much. "Oh yes, if I may?" and he looked at Lucy.

"We need help with these prisoners," Turias pointed out. "I think we should take them to Zandor. They might be connected to the outlaws he's hunting. I'll have a word with him on the V-phone in the caravan and get his advice."

None of this made any sense to Yani, V-phone, Zandor in the caravan?

Yani raised his voice and said as loudly as he could, "Why don't I just drown them?" and winked at Turias, who replied loudly "That's not a bad idea." More muffled protests came from the far side of the caravan.

Lucy put her head close to Yani's and whispered, "Ells don't kill if there is any hope of teaching people like that to live a better life." Here was another puzzle for Yani to think about. Turias disappeared into the caravan and various mutterings emerged.

"If this fellow Zandor is in there, why didn't he come out and fight those villains?" Yani wanted to know.

"My friend, wherever you've been living you've learnt nothing about civilized life." Pasco said. "Outside these protected areas, marvellous technologies are commonplace. Zandor isn't in the caravan but we can see and talk to him using a Video-phone."

Turias emerged to say that Zandor had advised leaving the prisoners at Lorca, only a few kilometres away. "The local guard will take charge of them and we could then travel faster. We are to meet him at Lahara in two days time."

During these two days Yani learnt something about this strange world he had entered. In return, he told them as much of his history as he could remember.

"Way back, I think there was a home near the sea, and family, and I dream about a white city... but then Mother, Dad and I travelled in a caravan, and then..." his mouth tightened... "I went off to play with a boy from a nearby gypsy camp. When I came back they were all buried under a rockfall."

Lucy laid a consoling hand on his shoulder. "Was your Mother an Ell, Yani?" she asked gently, concern in her eyes.

"I've no idea, I can hardly remember her face."

Lucy, who had only recently said goodbye to her mother, nodded silently, and sniffed back her own tears.

"Who is this Zandor you spoke to?" Yani asked Turias.

"The Lord Zandor is the senior Ell left on Earth. During the last few years the Ells have been departing steadily. Now only three or four are left. For some reason Zandor and his wife Arlinda offered to be the last to leave, so any disturbance will still get his attention. They'll organize our training when we reach Altania, so helping him at Lahara should be an interesting start. They've had some trouble there."

"Did you tell him about me?"

"No, I didn't really know enough about you and I knew he would ask too many questions. Let's surprise him!"

"What is this training you're going to do?" Yani asked.

Turias gazed ahead and sighed. "A few of us half-Ells, who are young enough not to have been totally swallowed up in Ell culture, still have a great love of Earth. We are volunteering to stay on here as Guardians, to counter any danger that remains."

"Danger?" Yani's eyes sparkled.

"Imagine how angry some humans were to have the Ells appear and reorganize everything. Even now, after all the restructuring, pockets of resentment exist. The humans can deal with that on their own, but problems could come from stolen Ell technology being used by villains hungry to acquire power. Wars could start up again."

"The Guardians would be needed to stop that?"

"If Ell technology has fallen into the wrong hands—yes."

Yani thought this was very interesting. Perhaps, if his mother had been an Ell then he too might become a Guardian.

He pointed his staff into the distance. "Zap!" he thought "Zap zap!" The power tempted him, he had enjoyed knocking down those men!

2

Lahara

Zandor grew impatient. He had ridden into Lahara on his magnificent stallion, ready to deal with their problem. However, everything was peaceful, with no sign of the brigands he had come to capture. Indeed, the only news of trouble had come from the three students travelling from the east. Turias had said little on the V-phone, but it appeared that they had coped well on their own.

Lahara's Lady Provost had asked for his help. Ten days ago, a stranger had arrived and suggested that, as the Ells had gone, Lahara would be sensible to seek the protection of his master, the Lord Draach, for a modest fee. Several Andalucian villages had already joined Draach's league; those who had refused found themselves pestered by bandits. Such a thing had not been heard of for centuries.

"It's outrageous," the Provost had said, greeting Zandor on his arrival. "Pure blackmail, I sent him packing of course, then the attacks started, crops burnt, equipment damaged, things like that. Now I've been warned that the town itself will be attacked if we don't join. That's when I called you."

"What have you done to defend the town?"

"Alerted all the farms in our district, called up the men trained for emergencies, but serious fighting is unknown. We only have hand weapons used in sporting events, bows, swords, etc—oh we have stun guns to deal with dangerous animals, but nothing else."

Zandor nodded. "I expect my three students to arrive this afternoon. They're coming cross-country from Valencia and had some trouble on the way. Perhaps they ran into some of Draach's men; I'll know more when they get here. Meanwhile I shall go and lunch at Bombard's hostelry."

Coming across the plain from the east, the white walls of Lahara on its hill could be seen from some way off. Both Yani's pony and Turias' stallion were tethered behind, while the other two horses pulled the caravan at a steady pace.

Yani was nervous. He had no idea how this Zandor would receive him. His scruffy appearance would not help; nevertheless he would stand up for himself. No one was going to order him about again, he had had enough of that in the village.

They clattered up the hill and along the cobbled street to the main square.

"There it is," announced Pasco, "Bombard`s Inn, just as he described it."

"The courtyard will take the caravan, then we can stable the horses," Turias said. "Can you all lend a hand."

That task completed, they entered the inn where the pompous figure of Bombard greeted them. "My young guests," he cried, "I`ve been expecting three of you--but you`re four, I see," and he looked doubtfully at the unkempt figure of Yani.

"Yes," Turias said briskly, "we are four now. Where is--?"

"The Lord Zandor is just finishing lunch. I`ll go and--"

"Don`t trouble," Pasco chipped in, "We`ll surprise him."

Unsure whether his important guest should be surprised, Bombard dithered as the youngsters swept past him. They identified the dining room by the tantalizing aroma of coffee.

Warned by the voices, Zandor had risen to his feet before they entered. Yani saw a tall, elegantly dressed figure surveying them with interest. He spoke in a deep voice.

"Turias, Pasco and Lucy, you are welcome! You will also be hungry I expect." Bombard hustled in.

"Can you find food for these young people, Bombard?"

"It`s all ready, my Lord, I`ll go and bring it in," and he scuttled off.

Zandor`s tone sharpened. "You have acquired a friend, Turias. I thought that you were advised not to involve any humans in--?"

Yani bristled. Did all old Ells jump to conclusions?

"I`ll leave," he said to Turias. "Thank you for—."

29

"No," shouted Pasco and Lucy together. "He saved us from the bandits and he must have Ell blood but knows nothing about it."

Zandor frowned. He looked at Yani's taught figure, poised for flight.

"Forgive me," he said, "I didn`t intend to be discourteous. Please sit down and tell me everything, but first give me your name. I am Zandor."

Yani looked warily at this man, who changed tack so swiftly.

"I am called Yani," he said, "and—."

Zandor shivered. He looked closely at the youngster.

"Yani?" he questioned.

"Yes, Yani."

"You`ve always been called Yani?"

"As long as I can remember. Why do you ask?"

"It`s just an unusual name, and one which…but forgive me again, you were about to tell me what happened."

"Perhaps I could tell you," Turias interrupted, "you`ll get a better picture."

The door opened and Bombard returned with platters of ham, cheese and bread together with wine, tumblers of juice and jugs of water. He laid these out on a side table, bowed and departed. Yani's eyes, his hair, his mannerisms, struck Zandor as familiar. A feeling grew inside Zandor that this Yani, this Yani might be…but his thoughts were interrupted as Turias started to tell of their encounter with bandits.

"Take your time," Zandor said, but the youngsters were so keen to tell him that they ate and spoke at the same time. Their adventure acquired some extra colour and Yani's role in saving them grew in the telling.

"Well!" said Zandor, looking intently at Yani, "it appears we are all in your debt. Would you mind telling me, as you have told your friends, everything you can remember about your early life."

However much he tried to still the excitement building inside him, the feeling grew stronger. He listened to Yani's words. The boy talked fluidly but cautiously, eyeing him suspiciously. He said something about being in a caravan, and his parents being killed in a rock fall. Zandor's head snapped up, and he lifted his hand. Yani went quiet.

"Turias, Pasco, Lucy, leave us." He spoke slowly, rising to his feet, his gaze fixed on Yani.

"Are you all right, Sir?" Turias asked, disconcerted.

"Yes, yes... Turias, I must speak with Yani alone— please?"

Turias, Pasco and Lucy looked at each other, rose to their feet and left the room. The door clicked shut, the only sound now was the crackling of the wood fire. Yani was not sure what to do. His heart began to race.

"Have I said something wrong?" he asked quietly.

"No...no." Zandor said in a kind voice. "Far from it. Come, sit by the fire, and finish your story." As Yani completed his tale, Zandor stared into the flames, deciding what to say.

At last he cleared his throat. "I shall tell you another story now, Yani. It's the best way to explain this to you," he said. "But first I really need some wine." He stood and poured himself a glass with a hand that shook.

He wanted to shout with joy, but this dirty, ragged, incredible urchin would not understand and probably bolt for the door. Yani sat crossed legged on the rug by the fire, waiting patiently till Zandor began his tale.

"Once I had a beautiful daughter. Her name was Elaire. She was the apple of my eye, my only child. At an early age for an Ell she wanted to marry a man called Alexander, a human. I was against it at first, because she was bright and clever, with a great life waiting for her when we left Earth. However, her powers of persuasion got the better of me and she married Alexander. Ah, they were a beautiful couple, full of love and laughter, and soon they had a son. I became a grandfather and this new role delighted me. I became very involved with the little boy. When he was three I gave him a puppy then, before he was four, I taught him to ride his first pony."

Zandor took a sip of wine and checked Yani's reaction. Maybe he could jog the boy's memory. Zandor smiled, the first smile Yani had seen, and it made him look strangely familiar. "Elaire and Alexander wanted to go on a trip to the Pyrenees in a caravan."

Yani frowned and said, "That is what my parents did," then realization dawned. "My mother—was she--?" he was trying to sort out this puzzle. "The hound, was it called Bob?" Yani was standing up now, his voice growing louder, more insistent, "I remember something, the pony, it was black, wasn't it?" Yani moved forward and grabbed Zandor's arms. "What does this mean? What are you telling me?" he demanded.

"Calm yourself, my boy, this is as difficult for me as it is for you." Zandor said, placing a hand on Yani's head.

"I know you, I know who you are!" Yani exclaimed, and pulled back to sit on his haunches, disbelief written all over his face.

"Yes you know me, Yani, or Yan t'Ell, as you were christened. Elaire called you Yani for short. We all did."

"Grandpa?" Yani whispered, looking up into Zandor's eyes that brimmed with tears.

"Yes, Yani, I am your Grandfather."

A smile that lit the room filled Yani's face. He did something he could not remember ever doing. Acting on impulse, he threw his arms around this man and hugged him as tightly as he could. Zandor, tears running down his face, couldn't speak. Yani, drawing back, found his voice first, and questions came pouring out.

"One at a time, my dear boy," Zandor eventually managed to say. "Ah Yani, little Yani, but look at you now! How have you lived? Where did you live? Now I know why it was I begged to be the last here. If I had not..." he shook his head, "no sense in dwelling on ifs."

He cleared his throat and stood up, "I have something in my saddle bag, please get it, it's on the hook by the door?" Yani did as he was asked, and Zandor pulled a leather case from the bag. He moved to the table, Yani beside him. Carefully he opened the case and pulled out some photographs. "I carry these with me wherever I go, Yani." There before him lay his parents, smiling up at him, even a picture of Yani as a toddler, one of him sitting on his Grandfather"s shoulders, one with Bob, so many others to look at and absorb. "There, you see how much you were loved, and are still loved, Yani?" Zandor said simply.

At this moment the door burst open and the Provost rushed in.

"They`re coming!" she cried, "a huge band of riders on the east road, about five hundred of them. I`ve called out the guard."

"What timing!" Zandor exclaimed, "All right, remain calm," he added to the Provost. "Yani, go and find the others, then head for the town gates, I want you to watch what I do from there." Zandor collected the photographs and put them away, then took up his cloak and staff. His deliberate movements made the Provost even more agitated. "Yani," Zandor said, raising an eyebrow at his grandson, who stood watching him, "go now."

CHAPTER THREE

1

Confrontation

Zandor headed for the stables, staff in hand, his dark cloak billowing out around him and his grey hair glinting in the sun. His black stallion stood at seventeen-two hands and together the two made a striking impression. Outside, the town was in chaos, people rushing around and shouting orders. Zandor walked sedately through it all, mounted his horse and set off calmly through the milling crowd. Somehow his ordered progress instilled an element of hope among the alarmed people.

Yani, having found the others, told them what they were to do. Outside they found the emergency force forming up, roughly forty Yani guessed, not nearly enough against five hundred. They ran down the street after Zandor as shutters closed over windows and the clang of wrought iron door-guards rang out on all sides. People who had never known danger in their lives, prepared for the worst. Yani caught snippets of shouts from all around, "There are five hundred." "No. Alain counted seven hundred." "More like a thousand." It was terrifying yet exhilarating to be part of this. It took the youngsters some time to reach the town gates; navigating through the confusion was no easy task.

"I can see him!" Lucy said, pointing dramatically to the foot of the hill. Yani, with a feeling of great pride, saw his grandfather riding his magnificent horse, solitary and powerful, straight at the approaching force.

"About two hundred, wouldn't you say?" he asked Turias, who nodded. "One against two hundred, it`s impossible? Right, I'm going down too," he announced, gripping his staff. "You were told to stay here," Turias grabbed Yani's shoulder. "He has great power and—."

34

"And he`s my grandfather. I`ve just found him and I`m not going to lose him now," Yani interrupted and, shrugging off Turias" grip, he squeezed through the gates and headed off at a run.

"Yani, listen to me—damn it," swore Turias, setting off after him.

"Yani`s gone crazy," said Pasco. "Lucy, stay here," and he brought up the rear, leaving Lucy at the gate.

Earlier that day, Draach had issued his instructions."This is our biggest bite yet," he told Brattas, his captain. "So far we have five villages. Lahara is a town, I admit, but the guard has only forty men who know nothing about fighting. They think they can hold out against us, but we`ll teach them. Take all our troops, kill the guards and anyone else who resists, then turn your men loose on the town. News will spread of what happens to those who oppose me. By the time you have finished with Lahara, people will fear the mere mention of my name."

The raiders were restless. Their greedy eyes shone at the mention of a full attack, especially the idea of an attack on a town renowned for its riches.

"We`ll have no trouble," Brattas had told them that morning as they prepared to head out to Lahara. "This is going to be our richest conquest ever."

They were getting close when Brattas became aware that one man on horseback was waiting in the middle of the road. His hope of a good fight died. They wanted to surrender, what a pity. Still, Draach would be pleased.

He held up his hand, and the cavalcade stopped. He eyed the tall man in front of him with suspicion. He didn`t look like someone about to surrender.

"Out of our way, old man, or—"

"Or?" Zandor asked.

Brattas moved his mount forward. He glanced at his sergeants, who were amused by the old man`s audacity, and replied, "Or I might send you flying off that fine horse, and take him for my own. He wouldn't look out of place in my

35

stable block." The men grinned and Zandor, patting his horse's neck, smiled in agreement.

"Indeed Kuzak is a fine animal, I can't disagree with you there. However, I shall give you all one chance to surrender. The other option is, how shall I put it, a little messy."

There was a roar of laughter from the men at this ridiculous statement. One of them let off a stun gun by mistake and Brattas threw up his hand for order.

Yani, halfway down the hill, heard the shot. He stopped in his tracks, and Turias almost ran into his back.

"They're shooting at Grandpa!" he panted. Turias, too much out of breath to speak, leant forward, hands on his knees, gasping and trying to say something to Yani. "Quick Turias, they're shooting at Grandpa," Yani repeated and set off again. Pasco appeared, leaping over a bush and skidding to a halt beside Turias.

"I heard a shot."

"Yes, yes, I know, I can hardly breathe but he's..." Turias waved his hand in the direction Yani had taken, "gone mad, calling Zandor "Grandpa."

"Right, ok, you catch your breath..." Pasco, slightly uncertain what to do, hovered by Turias, "I think I'd better help him." he decided and, with a last look at Turias, set off again. Turias, after more heavy breathing, pushed himself onwards after Pasco, muttering to himself.

Zandor surveyed the mocking men with something like pity. He lifted his staff, a streak of blue light shot out like a long whip, and moved skywards, across the top of the laughing raiders. Emitting high screeches like a violin, it expanded into a long translucent tent that fell down to surround the men. Brattas, cut off from his men, watched in amazement as the raiders tried vainly to escape the walls of their prison.

"What magic is this?" he demanded, turning to the old man.

"Not magic, just Ell science. I want to speak to you alone, Brattas," Zandor said, urging his horse nearer. "Now will you surrender?"

"Surrender? To whom? An old sorcerer... never!" but a look of fear was spreading across his face. How did this old man know his name? He drew his sword, Zandor's slow approach was making him nervous.

"Stay back," he warned.

"You are defeated and yet you still threaten me. You are a very brave man, however misguided."

"Who, or what, are you?" Brattas asked.

"I am Zandor," and he paused for effect. "I am Lord of the Ells in this land."

"Come any closer and you will be a headless Ell," Brattas managed to say, fearing he was fighting a losing battle. He had heard of Ells but had thought they were all dead, or gone.

"You have a choice, Brattas, to surrender to me, or to go back alone and face Draach. Do you think he will be pleased to see you?"

"My men, what will you do with my men?"

"Loyalty too, I am impressed. Do not be afraid for them, they are already disarming, look for yourself."

Brattas was loath to take his eyes off this Ell but couldn't help looking round and, sure enough, his men had not only dropped all their weapons but were taking off their armour too. Some were sitting on the ground, their heads in their hands and looking extremely distraught.

"What have you done to my army?" Brattas exclaimed.

"Ah, well, that's the messy bit." Zandor said. "Inside the bubble there is a disturbing vibration whereby they experience all the suffering and loss they have caused others. They are deeply, agonizingly, regretting their behaviour. Now they are free, a little lost, but free, and it is up to me to help them. They are no longer of any use to you."

Brattas was silent. His shoulders slumped. How could he return to Draach? Defeated by one man, Draach would have his head.

"I can see what you are thinking," Zandor said kindly. "Now drop that sword," he commanded. The hilt in Brattas's hand became unbearably hot, too hot for him to hold and he had to let it fall to the ground.

"Fight me! Fight me like a man!" he yelled, his voice breaking.

"I do not wish to fight you, I want to help you."

Brattas looked once more at his men, disarmed, disarmoured and watching him intently.

"This is what you call free? You've brainwashed my army! You Ells have interfered with us for too long."

"Not brainwashed, not at all. They are just experiencing the grief of every widow, every orphan, their killings have caused. Now tell me, what will it be?"

Brattas looked at his demoralized followers, then at this tall authorative figure smiling gently at him. Furious, he spat on the ground.

"You give me no choice, damn you. All right, I surrender." Brattas dismounted, took off his helmet, dropped it before him, along with the rest of his armour and stood, defiantly facing Zandor.

"Now you too should repent your killings," Zandor said, and a small blue light flared around Brattas. He sank to his knees, his hands rose to cover his face and his body started to shake. Racked by agony, grief and regret he beat his fists on the ground.

After some minutes Zandor spoke again. "I shall send an escort to guide you to Almeria where retraining and a better future awaits you. Time will heal your grief and you will find peace in your new life. I wish you well."

Zandor turned Kuzak back towards Lahara and it was then he noticed the three lads standing, staffs in hand, ready to come to his assistance. Behind them stood Lucy, gripping her staff tightly. He frowned.

"I thought I told you to—" he began, but then realized that perhaps he would have done the same had their roles been reversed. He smiled and said "Too much courage can create problems, but thank you for your support. These men are ready to go to Almeria at first light. For me, I need rest and

38

maybe some wine." Zandor did indeed look weary. Yani came over to Kuzak and took the reins.

"Grandpa, I saw everything. How did you—I mean what were you--?"

"Not now Yani, please. I`m exhausted."

They returned to a jubilant town, Zandor on Kuzak, being led by Yani, with Pasco, Lucy and Turias behind, full of questions about this relationship between Yani and Zandor. That evening, after supper, Zandor told the story of his daughter and Yani. His newfound friends looked at him in a different light.

Yani shook his head. "I`m still the same person I was before," he insisted, but still there was a new respect; this was the grandson of the legendary Zandor.

Lucy asked the obvious question. "How could Yani`s parents just disappear?"

Zandor`s shoulders fell. "We had arranged to speak no oftener than once a week on the V-phone, so some time passed before we became alarmed. After all, Alexander was very competent and Elaire had great powers. Natural disasters are rare. We searched for months while hope died slowly." He turned to Yani. "Could you remember nothing of life before the accident?"

Yani shook his head. "I suppose the horror wiped out happy memories. It was later I started to dream of a white towered city by the sea."

Zandor nodded. "Perhaps Yani and I should ride back to Altania together while you three follow in your own time. We have much to talk about." He raised an eyebrow and looked at Yani, "But only if you agree."

Yani looked at Turias, who smiled and said, "Of course you must go with your grandfather. You`ve a lot of catching up to do. We`ll meet up again in Altania."

On their journey Yani plagued Zandor with questions, starting with how he had subdued the raiders.

"Magic, Yani? No, not magic. While we Ells look very like humans, only a little taller and thinner, our brains are quite different. Our thoughts can cause things to happen and our special staffs augment this power. Remember how your anger shot fiery bolts—that's the beginning of your power. But you are not yet trained how to use it properly."

"Turias said that the Ells are all leaving Earth. Why must they leave?"

Zandor sighed. "There are only about four Ells left now. Indeed I do not wish to leave Earth at all, Yani. I have spent centuries here and I love this world and its people. But the Ell Council only allowed us to stay here long enough to sort things out. Now humans must show they can develop on their own, so I too must go—go and leave all this," and he waved his arm in a wide circle.

Yani looked at the long range of mountains ahead of them, still carrying traces of snow, shining under the morning sun.

"It's a strange thing," Zandor continued, "but almost two thousand years ago all this land was invaded by Moslems—the Moors—and for many years all the different religions lived and intermingled happily together. It was a golden age, rather like the type of civilization the Ells have created."

"Turias told me that Ells have flying machines and high speed transport systems. Why don't you use them now?"

Zandor smiled, "In a hurry to get there, are you? But we need time to talk. We could have used the tube system or flown, but that would have meant leaving our good steeds behind. Kuzak belongs back at Monteros, our family home. Besides," he added, "there's nothing I enjoy more than riding through this magnificent country."

"You said 'tube system.' What's that?"

"Long ago we installed a system of large underground vacuum tubes, linking towns and cities. Very fast and clean. The old transport systems have grassed over and disappeared. The only problem for the tubes is the occasional earthquake but they can withstand all but the most serious."

"Are there many tubes?"

"On the planet? Over a thousand."

"Wow."

40

Around noon on the third day they rode through a short tunnel near the top of a mountain pass.

"When we come out you will see Altania and the sea," Zandor said, just before they emerged into brilliant sunshine. They stood high up on a wide platform, the mountains stretching out on either hand as immense walls of grey. A huge vista lay before them. Very far below green fields reached away out to a city of white towers, "Altania, garden city of the Ells," murmured Zandor. Beyond it all, there lay the restless sea, blue, green and flecked with white. A breath of wind carried a new smell, one that instantly woke memories, the tang of the distant ocean.

Even further over the waters, faint in the distance, blue shadows proclaimed another land. Zandor pointed. "That`s Africa!" Looking down, not far below them, a lone eagle could be seen, quartering the skies in its search for food. Yani just gazed and gazed, till Zandor put a hand on his shoulder. "Do you think you`ll like it down there? Let`s go and meet your grandmother."

He turned and started down the track. For a long moment Yani remained spellbound. Joy and memories flooded his heart. The long years of exile and loneliness were gone; at last he had come home.

2

Altania

Yani paced the beach. Spray, blowing on the sea wind, soaked his clothes and coated him white, but the boy barely noticed. The spring storm that had raged overnight had gone, but its fury remained in the sea, just as the turmoil from his meeting with Grandma Arlinda raged in his heart.

Her words still rang in his ears. Zandor and Yani had arrived at Monteros, the family home, the previous evening. Riding across the plain from the mountains, they saw dark clouds pouring in from the west. "Faster," cried Zandor,

41

urging his stallion on. Just as they clattered into the courtyard the heavens opened.

"In here, Yani," cried Zandor, riding straight into the stables. A burly man appeared from a side door calling "Welcome home," then he saw Yani behind and his whole face lit up.

"It's Yani!" he roared. "Martha woman, come quickly."

A plump figure emerged. "For heavens sake, Rob, must you make so much noise? Anyone would think—" her voice broke off as she caught sight of the boy dismounting from Hardy, then, "Yani! My baby, my boy," she shrieked, in a sound that totally drowned Rob's efforts.

Dismounting, Yani found himself enveloped in her embrace and was too startled to move. Zandor laughed and explained. "This is Martha, your nurse when you were small. Rob here is her husband. He manages everything at Monteros."

"We could hardly believe the news when Arlinda told us."

"Yes, Rob, She'll want to see the boy. We'd better not keep her waiting."

Yani followed Zandor through a wide doorway. Inside, a lady stood to greet them as they entered. Arlinda had a presence to match Zandor's. Tall and imperious, she watched Yani through eyes betraying her joy. A tentative smile quivered and she opened her arms wide.

"Yani, my little Yani, come to Grandma," and she wrapped the boy in a fierce hug. At last she released him, but only to inspect him at arm's length.

"You must be starving, supper's ready, come with me." She barely noticed Zandor's smile, all her attention focussed on the boy, husbands didn't matter.

After they had eaten, the questions started. Arlinda wanted to know everything Yani could recall about the accident that had killed his parents.

"Bob and I had gone to see Jaco, a boy from the gypsy camp and when I got back there was only a mountain of stones." Memory silenced him for a moment, then he

42

continued, "Bob must have gone back to the gypsies and alerted them. Georgio Sandor, their leader, told me later they had to drag me away from these stones. I had been trying to dig underneath with my hands."

Arlinda shook her head as she imagined the scene, then asked, "What did the gypsies do for you?"

"They cared for me for about three years, but they knew I came from the south. Just as they were leaving for the Camargue they met up with Mika, a traveller, whom they trusted. He thought he knew the white city, which was all I could remember of my past. Mika offered to take me there and we set off. After several days we reached his old village, then everything went wrong."

"And you spent seven years in that terrible place, with no friend but Mika? Did he teach you to read, count and speak properly?"

"Mika taught me a little. He said I was a quick learner, but mostly I learnt from my dream lady."

"Dream lady? What lady?"

"The one who speaks to me every night in my dreams."

Arlinda froze in disbelief. She tried to speak but her throat had dried.

She stared at Yani, then at Zandor, who had jumped to his feet. At last her voice returned. "His dreams," she croaked at Zandor, "his dreams. Don`t you realize what they mean?"

Zandor and Yani stared at her. Tears ran down her cheeks; she shook them off angrily as she paced the floor.

"Elaire must still be alive!" she cried. "This boy can read, write, count and will have many other skills. Where do you think he got them, out of thin air?" She waved her arms and gave an exasperated sigh. "In his dreams, of course, as every Ell child is taught by its mother till puberty, but only from a living Ell mother. Elaire must be alive! All these years we mourned her, while all the time she has been alive, teaching him as he slept. Our daughter is alive!"

"Mother? Alive?" Yani cried. "My Mother is alive?" By now he had memorized Zandor's pictures of his mother. "Where is she?"

Zandor paced the room, striking his fist into his left hand and muttering. "I should have seen it too," he reproached himself. "But where is she? Who has the strength to hold an Ell against her will?"

"Whoever it is must be dealt with, but how do we find her?"

Zandor leant on the table and looked straight into Arlinda's eyes. "I shall begin a search at once. Meanwhile Yani has skills to learn before he—."

Yani glared at him. "I'm coming too," he announced defiantly.

"No, you're staying here," Arlinda stated, "First of all we have to search an enormous area to pinpoint where she might be. You can't help there. Also, you must be properly trained or we'll lose you again."

"No you won't!" Yani shouted.

"Really?" Arlinda replied quietly and, raising a hand, pointed it at him.

He struggled to move and found he couldn't. She held his gaze and, as the minutes passed, he began to realize the sense in what she said. He had to bide his time, learn these strange Ell skills, and not rush off unprepared.

At last her grip eased and he could move again. She put her arms round him. "Yani, my darling, you see even I can make you powerless. Think what an enemy could do. He holds your mother prisoner, and she has great power, while you have only a little as yet. Now, while your Grandpa starts his enquires, I shall begin your instruction.

"One other thing we must do is to call the Widow Grimstone and let her know you are safe. She's a fine woman and I should like to speak to her myself."

Later that evening Arlinda called the Widow and explained that Yani was her grandson.

The Widow was delighted. "I knew there was something special about him and I`m so pleased he`s found his family. I worried about him going off on his own but he was very determined. Thank goodness he`s safe now."

Yani slept soundly that night then, early next morning after breakfast, Arlinda said, "Now you and I are going to fly." Yani`s eyes lit up.

A gleaming oval machine sat in the courtyard. Some four metres long, its clear domed hood swung open as they approached. Inside were two pairs of seats and a number of controls on a panel at the front.

"This is my little bubble flyer and it will take us to our apartment in Altania.

"It can fly? Why are there no wings? Birds have wings."

"That's one of the many things you`ll learn."

"I`ve seen things like this in my dreams, but not how they work."

"Well it`s quicker than riding," she smiled, as they settled themselves inside and closed the hood. She laid her hand on a lever and pressed it down.

There was a faint humming sound, then the ground fell away below them, though Yani felt no movement, and a vista of green lands and blue sea opened before his eyes. Straight ahead lay Altania, city of his dreams, shining white in the sun. Its circular wall had four entrance points. Outside, well-tended fields stretched far into the distance. As they approached, Yani noted that the slender elegance of the buildings created an impression of height, though in fact none were more than seven stories high. They were interlaced with gardens, tree lined paths and many fountains.

"It`s more like a big garden than a city," Yani said, as they landed on the roof of a six-storey building in the middle. Climbing out, Yani, still exhilarated by the flight, asked "Why didn`t Grandpa fly to Lahara?"

"He loves this country and grabs any excuse to go riding in the mountains. In any case, we try to keep flights over the protected lands to a minimum. He also wanted to deal with these men from horseback, not overpower them with machinery and weapons."

Yani laughed, "He certainly overpowered them."

Arlinda nodded. "Now come with me, our living apartment is on the top floor," and she lead the way down a flight of stairs and opened a solid teak door. Inside, she put a hand on Yani's shoulder. "This will be your home till you start at college. Now, let me tell you about bees," she said.

Yani's face grew hot, "Grandma, I already know about the 'birds and bees'. Living in that village—."

"Ha!" Arlinda scoffed, "Not those bees, this is quite different. You see, when the Ells saw the problems Earth had, the first tool they needed was a tiny bee-like device. They used them to monitor thousands of places over several years and send back pictures and sound, without being detected. That's how we learnt what was going on and who the troublemakers were. Those bees are the eyes and ears of whoever controls them. They are barely visible and the best spying invention ever made."

"But how do you control them?" Yani asked.

"I'll show you," Arlinda said. "Would you like to fly one?"

"Oh yes!" exclaimed Yani. Arlinda took him to a circular room without windows and explained. "That big chair is the controller's seat. Your hands guide the movements of the bee; you can listen and watch when wearing that headset. Try it, a bee's on the roof so you can start from there. What the bee sees is also transmitted onto the walls of this room." She placed a helmet over Yani's head and everything went dark.

Arlinda pressed a switch and at once Yani felt he was standing on the roof looking towards the sea. Arlinda guided his hands to the simple controls, "pull here and the bee rises, pull here and it will go right or left as you wish--"

Already Yani was experimenting, his breath coming faster and faster as he seemed to swoop around the city.

"This is terrific," he shouted, as his bee shot down avenues of trees, then soared up high above Altania's elegant, filigree towers. He turned towards the sea where a remaining angry

46

squall darkened the sky. A shower of rain lashed down, then the sun broke through again. Heart racing, Yani dived his bee down towards the shore, hurtling along just above the breakers. A kaleidoscope of colours dazzled his eyes as the sunlight sparkled into a myriad tiny rainbows along the breaking waves. "This is fantastic," he yelled.

Smiling, Arlinda left him to develop his skill as a bee flyer. She gave him a good hour before returning to shake his shoulder. "Come back to the real world now Yani. You've learned enough for one day. Go and walk down to the shore and get some fresh air. Feel the sand beneath your feet as you did many years ago."

Walking the beach in reality, Yani was exhilarated by the sea-tang and thunder of the breakers. He thought about the last three weeks: his escape from Polonia, the loss of Bob, finding friends at last, discovering that Ells were special and not dirty, and then reunion with his amazing and distinguished grandparents. Above all, his mother was alive somewhere. Resolution firmed in his mind. Yes, he would learn Ell skills but then, afterwards, nothing and no one would stop him rescuing his mother.

The soothing song of the sea, the cry of the gulls and the clean salt air gradually calmed his mind. At last he turned and walked back towards Altania's white towers shining in the afternoon sun.

CHAPTER FOUR

1

The Pyrenees

"I, Krask, Count Aranda, write this as a guide for my two daughters should I die in this struggle. For forty years I have carried on the work of my forebears, opposing the interfering Ells and the effete culture they have imposed on mankind. Soon the last ones will depart and our time will come. I have done my best for my people, supporting those disadvantaged by their rejection of Ell teaching. I have built bases in the caverns of our mountain and its neighbour, Mahmoural. There our weapons and power grow, waiting for the day when we shall take control and restore human dignity and freedom to this shackled, bamboozled planet.

We need strength and knowledge of their advanced technology. Little they will leave to humans when they go, so it is up to us to seize what we can and bend it to our purpose. Once every year or so I have kidnapped a scientist whose knowledge might help us. These disappearances have been disguised as natural accidents so that no suspicion is aroused. Though these prisoners work for us, most of them do so unwillingly and so we must learn even more of Ell technology.

This is why I have sent Estella, my youngest daughter, to study in the heartland of our foes. She has great talent in things scientific and will create weapons and tools for our use. Never forget the insult offered to your ancestor who was abandoned by her Ell lover when she was expecting their child. Ells are not to be trusted. The glorious history of our planet has been buried and forgotten by these interlopers. They told us lies, that there was no hope for us without their help and that Earth's ecology was being destroyed. All lies.

At least from that indiscretion of my grandmother, we have the benefit of some Ell longevity. They live ten times the human span, though they did double that, the one good thing

48

they brought. With luck we should manage a few hundred years.

However, it would be of help if we can add to the number of Ell genes in our family. For years I have been able to keep an Ell woman captive, thanks to my scientists` development of a collar that blocks transmission of anger from their powerful brains. Even so I dare not touch her without her agreement. Collared though she is, she has the ability to kill us both. I continue to try and persuade her to bear me a child but so far she has refused. A better hope is for my younger daughter to ensnare a young Ell. A child born to them and trained to our ways, would become a mighty weapon for the future.

To Zenia, my fierce warrior daughter, falls the task of attacking the soft civilization the Ells have created. Unused to warfare, they will crumble easily. Around the world there are still many small, scattered communities that have been left to their own devices. Most are in remote, mountainous regions, or on small islands. I have established links with several of these and from such contacts we shall build our strength. In my safe you will find the information needed to contact these groups. Do not trust the gypsies however, they hold themselves apart from any outside influence."

Krask laid down his pen. Writing was not his forte but if anything happened to him, Zenia should have some guidance from him. He didn`t doubt her ability to keep control, she was determined, cruel and without scruples. He sealed the letter in an envelope addressed to Zenia and added "To be opened in the event of my death."

The blood of the old conquestadores ran in his veins and, being a huge man, he usually overcame any opposition by force and fear—but there was one exception.

As he did every month, he went to visit his priceless captive, a woman of pure Ell blood, kept in specially designed quarters deep inside the neighbouring mountain. Through the one-way glass he watched her for some time. Slim and erect, tawny hair hanging down her back, she moved with an easy grace. Her face, fine boned and elegant, had a serenity and directness about it that always irritated Krask. Not one of his threats had been able to disturb her equanimity.

He rang a bell announcing his presence, before opening the glass door.

"My Lady Elaire," he said, and bowed.

"Count Aranda," she acknowledged him calmly, while her dark blue eyes inspected him as if he were an interesting specimen in a laboratory.

"Have you given any further thought to my repeated proposal, to set you free once you have married me and given me a son."

"You know that is something I will never do. Allow me to lay my hands on you and, even collared as I am, you would feel the power of an Ell."

It was like being in a cage with a lioness, Krask thought. He always kept a long stick in his hand when visiting her just in case....but he enjoyed the danger.

"Come, that would kill us both" he said. "Have you forgotten it was I who ransomed you from the bandits who attacked your family? Besides you had a human husband once—"

"Do you imagine that I would consider taking you in his place? Anyway I believe you have several children by different mothers. Content yourself with them."

"Only my two daughters matter. Their mother was remarkable, like you," and for a moment Krask's voice softened as he recalled Miriam, the one woman he had really loved.

Sensing his change of mood, Elaire asked, "Why do you persist in this campaign against the Ells. We shall all be gone, quite soon—"

"But leaving a contented, supine planet as your legacy," responded Krask. "Mankind's lot is discontent, dispute, struggle, out of which grows true strength. You have created an ordered civilization, every child taught to develop its best talents, rather than fight to find its way. You have reduced population levels to a fraction of what—"

"The planet couldn't sustain its teeming masses." Elaire pointed out quietly, only irritating her captor more.

"So you tell us, fairy tales, false history, I don't believe it. Just an excuse for you to lord it over us. We have always managed—"

"To create war, pollution, misery? Yes, these things mankind did very well."

Krask's face became red. "You arrived uninvited, spied on what we were doing, then interfered in every aspect of our life. Where are the huge cities now, our great industries, our transport systems? Shrunk or gone, that's what—"

"They became unnecessary. You were destroying the planet and millions were starving. We brought free energy from the sun and matter transformers to produce all the machinery needed. We taught each generation religious tolerance and all children to create, not destroy. Now sports and arts have replaced wars."

Krask shrugged. "To make great steel, stress is necessary. Our best inventions were born in times of war. Consider our great artists, mostly those who suffered."

"There are better ways to achieve such things. All this stress you have brought me, holding me here, keeping me from my child, what has that achieved?"

Krask pointed to the stack of paintings Elaire had created during the lonely years. "These perhaps? Why not a child for me?"

"You know the answer to that. Besides, I painted before."

"Each month I shall ask you again. Eventually you will agree. I bid you good day," and, once again frustrated, Krask departed.

CHAPTER FIVE

1

The Intervention

In Altania, Yani, Turias, Pasco and Lucy met in a small hall at the University. Five helmets lay on a side table. Arlinda, their instructress, arrived with another student in tow. Pasco smiled at him and the newcomer grinned back.

"Learning here is easy," Arlinda said. "Most of it is done by watching events via these virtual reality helmets. Sit down and put them on."

She ensured that each helmet was properly adjusted. "The first thing you will see is the beginning of the Intervention, some four hundred years before. Humans had an attempt at world government called The United Nations. That is where the Ells announced their intentions."

All five switched on the helmets and immediately had a viewpoint floating high above a huge debating chamber. Angry voices were raised and charges and counter-charges flew across the floor. Suddenly a great gong rang out and a strange humming sound stilled the voices. A figure, about five metres tall, appeared from nowhere in the middle of the forum. It wore a robe shimmering with subtle colours. Its stern face had fine features and deep-set commanding eyes. A mane of thick grey hair proclaimed its seniority. The delegates were stunned, almost forgetting to breathe.

It raised its hand and spoke in a clear voice. "I am Zelton, an emissary of my people, the Ells. We have come here to resolve your problems." A group of security guards appeared, alerted by the gong, but stopped, uncertain what to do.

"Perhaps the Secretary General will allow me to continue?" said Zelton, turning and bowing courteously.

"You certainly have the floor, whatever you are," the Secretary General managed to reply.

Zelton smiled slightly and said "Do not be alarmed by my apparent size, what you see is a holographic projection. I am actually only two metres tall."

"As of this moment, my race, the Ells, assume control of Earth's chaotic affairs. Wars will end and areas of conflict will be calmed. Agitators and terrorists have long since been identified and are now being removed to centres of our choosing.

"Gradually the problems of over-population and pollution will be solved. We shall nurse Earth's ecology back to health and encourage people to live in peace and in harmony with nature.

"We Ells have greater powers than you can imagine: limitless energy supplies from the sun, climate control, provision of food and clean water for everyone, education for every child; the benefits we bring are many."

An irate delegate interrupted, "We don't need you here. We are solving our own problems and—"

Zelton's eyebrows rose. "Really? Exactly where are the various terrorist groups? How will you defuse these endless religious hatreds? What are your plans for solving pollution, famine, disease—shall I go on? We have monitored events for decades and know exactly how serious things are. It has been rather like watching an asylum run by the inmates. No Sir, you have had your chance and failed."

"There is another reason we have come. Millions of years ago our ancestors visited this planet. Less wise than we are now, they introduced some genetic changes. Humankind today is the result of that well intended interference and the Ell Central Council believes we have a duty to help you, our distant cousins, in your difficulties.

"All national leaders and people in authority are receiving this message simultaneously. You will, of course, wish to refer to your governments for instructions but have no doubt, from this day forward this will become a better world. I shall return here every day at midday to answer any questions you may have. I bid you farewell!"

The scene faded and the students took off their helmets. They stared at each other. Wars, pollution, famine—what were they?

"What happened next?" Lucy asked.

"Widespread alarm which was gradually calmed, then centuries of restructuring, the introduction of Ell schools—but that's enough for today," Arlinda replied.

On the way out, Pasco introduced the newcomer to his friends. "This is Ragore," he said. "We got to know each other when I was here last year. Ragore's a keen sailor—he's also a budding playboy, so beware."

Ragore, hazel-eyed, brown haired and sturdily built, smiled warmly as he shook Yani's hand. Having grown up in Altania he was already well acquainted with its many charms. Though only a year older than Yani, with his Ell genes he looked like a young man of seventeen.

"I've found a great place to spend the evening" he told Yani, keen to introduce this rather serious looking boy to some fun. "There's a great group of guitarists and dancers."

"Don't be led astray by this bon viveur," laughed Pasco. "Even last summer his reputation was wild. He had just discovered wine, followed quickly by girls. Frankly, I'm surprised to see him still around."

"So this beautiful girl is the sister you told me about," said Ragore, ignoring Pasco's digs. "Lucy, I am delighted to meet you at last. Pasco's lucky to have such a lovely sister."

He laid a friendly hand on her shoulder. "Now about these guitarists, why don't you and I—?"

"You're wasting your time, Ragore. I've already warned her—"

"But I'm quite old enough to make up my own mind, dear brother," Lucy chipped in. "That sounds a great idea, Ragore. Why don't we all go tonight after our last class."

"But I've no money!" Yani stammered.

"Never mind, Turias will pay," Pasco retorted.

"You know, for a little chap he hides his money well," Turias said. "Deep pockets and short arms."

Yani persisted, "What do I do for money?"

"No problem, my young wanderer. Arlinda asked me to take you to the student`s office now. They`ll fit you with a bracelet like mine." Turias held out his arm and Yani could just make out a very thin strand of some metal round his wrist.

"How does that—"

"Supply money? Easy! It allows you to pay your bills from the credit given to you each week. You can also draw cash if you are going outside the city. You just stick your hand—oh, come on and I`ll show you."

Ragore listened to this with amazement. "You mean you`ve never had a bracelet? How did—" Lucy slipped one arm through Ragore`s and the other through Pasco`s "Let Yani go with Turias. You come with us and we`ll tell you everything that happened.

2

Changes

Yani still puzzled over his conversation with Arlinda, when she had spoken of his visit to the Tower.

"Puberty?" he had asked. "What`s that?"

Arlinda smiled. "It's the bridge from childhood to adulthood. In humans it takes years and the emotional and physical changes are very disturbing. Some have even said it`s like being shackled to a lunatic! However, for those with Ell genes, it all happens in four weeks and these should be spent at the Tower. During this time your body will grow by two years. You will feel powerful, restless desires and your mind will flood with conflicting emotions. Eventually this passes, but it`s a tumultuous time. Dr Macgregor will give you advice which should help. We shall fly by bubble"

"The one you brought me here in? You never explained how they can fly."

"Always curious. You`ll learn about anti-gravity systems when you come back. I should tell you that Macgregor`s a diehard Scotsman, but don`t be put off by that. He is an excellent teacher and has some Ell ancestors, that`s why he`s lived such a long time."

Macgregor duly arrived, wearing tartan trews, a short red beard and a confident air. He bristled with energy. "You come along with me, laddie, and I`ll get you sorted out in no time."

Unsure whether or not he wanted to be "sorted," Yani followed Macgregor to his office. The Doctor walked to his desk and fixed Yani with a bright eye.

"Your Granny`s told me a bit about you and I`m sure you`ll manage this business just fine. It`s a long time since I went to the Tower—my Grandad was an Ell—but I remember it fine. Now look at this."

He went across to a side table where a pot of wax simmered over a burner. Beside it were several differently shaped moulds.

"When you start puberty you are soft like this wax, when you leave it you`ve chosen your mould, the wax has hardened and is fixed for the rest of your life."

"You mean it`s impossible to change later?"

"Not impossible, later experiences have impact, but any fundamental change means being melted all over again—not easy at all, so choose carefully now."

"I`ll choose the best one," Yani said confidently.

"Aha, but how? You see the Tower has a weird staircase that climbs through several floors. You too have different "floors," body, mind and spirit. Choose to stop at the lower levels and when you come back from the Tower after a month, your character will remain on that floor."

Yani frowned, "So I should aim higher?"

Macgregor laughed, "Just do your best, laddie. Now there`s more I`ve to teach you and some tests to do."

Six days later, Arlinda asked Macgregor, "Is the lad ready?"

The Doctor nodded. "He`s a fast learner, but his biological clock is ticking. I think you should get him to the Tower by tomorrow."

"Right," said Arlinda, "We shall leave immediately."

Within the hour Yani found himself in Arlinda"s bubble flyer, the white towers of Altania dwindling behind them. They soared high and fast into the blue, high above the clouds, which thickened to form a mysterious floor shining below. North and west they flew, Arlinda throwing occasional glances at the expectant boy beside her.

"No questions, Yani?"

"Dr Macgregor explained so much I am still digesting it all. It's exciting but not easy to imagine. He said that afterwards I will be able to become a father!" Yani stopped for a moment, then added, "But I don't have to immediately, do I?"

Arlinda laughed, "No, Yani, not immediately. I rather think you are going to be too busy."

Yani stared ahead, remembering Lula. "And girls may not like me," he said softly.

Arlinda smiled. "That's always possible; better wait and see."

Yani nodded then returned to the present. "Where is this Tower? We've come a long way already."

"It's nature has always been a mystery. All I can tell you is that the entrance to it is on an island of great beauty in the Hebrides but, whether the Tower is entirely of this world or not, no one can say. It seems to exist in another dimension, and can be reached from different places."

Yani found this impossible to imagine, and then there was its weird inside to worry about. Noticing his concern, Arlinda added, "I, too, was taken there by my father a very long time ago. You'll be all right."

They flew on, the cloud cover fell behind, and Arlinda brought the craft down till they were almost skimming the waves. The sun was quite low in the west when, ahead of them, Yani saw blue mountain peaks appearing. The craft gained height again till many islands could be seen scattered about, small and large, some with jagged peaks, others flat, while off to their right, great ranks of snow-capped mountains formed an impressive mainland.

The colours were brilliant, a sapphire sea running into emerald flanked sea-lochs, with myriads of shades from aquamarine to deep purple. Here and there, beaches of white sand and translucent water looked so inviting that Yani yearned to land there and dive into the sea. Arlinda guessed what he was thinking.

"It's much colder than it looks, Yani. Up here in the north, winter holds on."

As the evening deepened, they flew up along the largest island they had yet seen. Leaving a wild group of dark blue mountains on their left, they continued to the north end of the island where, high among some cliffs, Yani saw a strange tower. It was not made of anything familiar; it seemed slightly translucent and appeared to be wrapped in mist. He had the feeling that if he blinked it might disappear.

Arlinda landed their craft on some cropped grass from which a path ran up towards the tower.

"Here you are, Yani. Good luck! The next bit you must do on your own. I shall return for you in a month."

Suddenly the boy felt very much alone. He had just found his family and now was to be alone again. A lump rose in his throat and his eyes pricked with tears.

"Grandma!" was all he managed to say.

Arlinda put her arm round him.

"It's all right, Yani," she said, "Remember, we all love you but you can't remain a boy forever."

Yani nodded and climbed out, then he realized: "but I've no food, no fresh clothes!"

"The Tower will provide," his grandmother assured him, "Yani, good luck!"

CHAPTER SIX

1

The Tower

The tower stood proudly before him, ancient, forbidding, sinister in appearance, yet tempting him to accept its challenge. Mist swathed the lower part and in the fading light of day, it appeared a strange and eerie place. A shiver ran down Yani's spine as he climbed the path, a shiver of both excitement and fear. He sensed every blade of grass, every scent, every whisper on the wind. His legs began to feel heavy, even after only a short distance. Like wading through water, simply picking up each foot took a great deal of effort. His breath quickened but he soldiered on as if in a dream, trying to walk to the end of a corridor with the door at the end coming no nearer.

It seemed to take forever to reach the mist, but as soon as it was around him the heavy feeling in his legs vanished, and he leapt forward in a rather clownish fashion. A laugh escaped him before he broke into a jog, his body now feeling weightless. The mist was thick and he tried to slow down, visibility was only arms' length, and going quickly was dangerous. He almost collided with the entrance, then his hands, pushing against the cold stone pillars, steadied him. He took deep breaths, peering to see where he had ended up. He didn't want to be the first Ell to take a wrong turning and end up at the back door.

Double doors swung slowly open and, with a sigh of relief, Yani saw he had indeed found the right entrance. Inside, a copious circular hall welcomed him with a vigorous fire roaring up a central chimney. Yani entered cautiously, but with his head held high, alert and ready for anything that might happen. The doors closed behind him—now there was no turning back.

He stood for a time familiarizing himself with his new surroundings. A huge stone pillar stood in the middle of the hall. It held the wide fireplace and served both as a chimney and the central support for a staircase, which wound its way anti-clockwise up into the dark. Hanging tapestries dressed the bare walls with scenes of woods and temples.

In front of the fire, a long oak table greeted him with a mouth-watering supper. Silver goblets and plates glistened in candlelight, and the rich furnishings made it look welcoming and comfortable. Yani sighed with relief then wandered around exploring this fascinating room. He discovered a bathroom with fresh clothes laid out for him, so he showered and changed before eating. After his meal, suddenly tired, he lay back on the sofa, pulled up a blanket, and fell asleep to the soothing sounds of the fire.

When he woke from a deep sleep, it took some moments to remember where he was. During the night the supper dishes had been removed and fruit left in its place. He rose, dressed, and munched an apple, becoming more apprehensive about the staircase waiting for him. "This won't do," he said out loud, took a deep breath and approached the first step.

"Here I go," he thought and, wanting to close his eyes but not daring to, he took one step. A tremor ran right through him. He paused to let it pass before taking the second step. Another even more intense shock followed. He continued to climb slowly, and after each step a shock pulsed through him, first his legs, then his torso, going right down his arms to his fingers. Every muscle, every hair on his body quivered, as if he was waking up to his physical form for the first time. The higher he climbed the stronger a sense of anticipation grew; something different approached. Sounds came from above where the staircase disappeared into a dark mist. He kept going, his heart pumping, the noises getting louder and louder. The light around him faded to complete darkness.

"One more step, Yani," he urged himself, took it, and burst into bright sunlight. He stopped abruptly, his arms swung out to keep his balance and, looking down, he checked that his feet were still on the stone stairs. Before him lay a wide beach, with children laughing and playing, swimming and surfing. Some were eating ice-cream, as they watched their friends playing a ball game, while the younger ones built sandcastles.

Yani stood detached, watching them, regret flickering in his heart. These children were so happy playing together. He thought of himself when he was that age, friendless and slaving on Jord`s farm.

"Stop feeling sorry for yourself," he muttered. He was different from these carefree kids, who beckoned him to join them. He was happy for them, but his days for playing were now over. He smiled at them, and waved goodbye, before turning back to the spiral staircase.

"Onwards and upwards, Yani," he said out loud—then stopped abruptly. Something had happened to his voice. It was lower than before. He tried it again, and yes, it was definitely an octave or two lower. "Good grief! I sound just like Zandor!" He chuckled and started climbing once more, humming quietly and enjoying his new, mellow tones. No more than twenty more steps brought him back into darkness and he braced himself for what was to come next.

Music and brightness pierced the gloom, coming from an archway opening into a vast, softly lit hall, full of people laughing and drinking, some smoking, some dancing. The ladies wore shimmering dresses, revealing and elegant and the young men looked very grand in their party gear. It was intoxicating and exciting to see but Yani stood his ground, wary of leaving the stairs.

"Yani!" A young lady, delicate features framed by a halo of blonde hair, smiled straight at him. Her eyes sparkled with delight. Every nerve quivering, Yani couldn`t take his eyes off her. She did not walk, she floated towards him and he was fascinated. He tried to reply but his voice was lodged in his throat and he, to his utter disgust, was blushing. What was wrong with him?

"Darling," she cooed, delighted to see his flushed face, "we`ve been waiting for you. Come in, have some champagne, relax and smoke a little?" Her skin glistened like silk, and her perfume filled the space between them. She was moving closer and closer to him and he was melting towards her. She was irresistible, his heart thumped, he was utterly confused, yet somehow his feet remained planted to the stone slabs that bordered the red carpet.

"What is this? Don't you want to party, darling?" she frowned, "Don't you want to spend some time with me, Yani?" Her face was almost touching his, her arm was winding its way around his, her fingers caressed his hand. He wanted to bend down towards those red lips and kiss her, but something stopped him. Something Dr Macgregor had said snapped into his head, shaking him awake. At last he found his voice.

"First you must show me the one who came before me."

"He's somewhere here," she said vaguely, sweeping her arm to take in the crowd, "ah yes, over there on the sofa."

Yani followed her pointed finger and saw a very sad figure of a man. Slouched on a sofa, his tie undone, his overweight body stretching his stained dinner suit, the fellow was obviously the worse for drink.

"He used to be so lively, but look at him now!" and she screwed up her face before flashing another smile. Her eyes sparkled with mischief. "Come off that silly staircase and we can really have a good time. Try my magic cigarette, it'll make you feel marvellous."

Yani pulled his fingers free, and took a step back. He smiled kindly at her. "For how long do you think we would have fun? Is fun all that matters? You are lovely, but eventually I would become like him, then you would become bored with me too."

"Never, Yani," she said, but the sulky look on her face told its story, she had failed to lure him. He smiled regretfully at her and turned to go, determined not to look back. She called after him but he kept climbing until he could no longer hear her voice.

Again it grew dark and darker still. The stairs became so large that Yani had to reach out with his hands for the next step then haul himself up onto it.

"It's like climbing a mountain," he thought, as he struggled on.

The voices of Marc and Lula mocked him. "Look at the little rat, he'll never make it. Why doesn't he throw himself off and end it all?"

He forced himself to concentrate. "Go away, leave me alone!"

"You'll always be alone. You're a failure, you'll never succeed, you haven't the strength."

"I managed to beat you two anyway," he muttered through gritted teeth.

Pain shot through his arms each time he pulled his body up another step and each time he had to rest for longer. "I will conquer this tower, then I'll go and find Mother," he promised, and gathered his strength for yet one more effort.

At last some light returned and the staircase reverted to normal. Three steps more brought him to the next level. To his right lay a library where people studied manuscripts. On his left Yani saw laboratories where whitecoated figures peered into test tubes, while others weighed and mixed various compounds.

An ascetic, but well dressed elderly individual greeted him.

"Thank goodness you resisted that siren below," he said, "She has lured too many promising candidates to their degradation but you have too fine a mind to waste your talents there. Here you can obtain mastery of all earthly sciences, exercise your brain to its limits, enlighten your people by your insight and guide them with your knowledge. It's a fascinating life—come and join us."

Again Yani asked to see the one who had accepted before his arrival.

"My name is Foska, Professor of too many things to tell you now. I have worked here for eighty-two years. I was the latest recruit," and Foska bowed.

"What else do you do besides research and study? Have you any children?" Yani enquired.

"Oh, no time for any of that. Affairs of the mind keep me fully occupied."

"Thank you," said Yani, "but I think I must go on." To be buried deep in study and have nothing else? That was not for him, he had more immediate things to do.

He climbed a few more steps and emerged into sunlit open country. The staircase went no further and Yani felt free to walk off the top tread. As he did so, a tall upright military figure appeared on his left.

"Congratulations young man, a potential leader if ever I saw one, excellent character. Capital! Capital! Allow me to introduce myself. I am General Pinner, though my men call me the Panther. Swift and deadly. Now look here, young Yani, I believe you are just what we need to sort out these wretched misguided humans. They need a master – a Master – to keep them in good order. Wouldn't you like to do that?"

"Well," said Yani, "I...." but the General carried on: "Some problems remain. Let me show you what they can get up to." He waved his hand.

A mountain appeared in front of them, then the picture zoomed into a large cave. Beyond, deep in the mountain, slaves worked at fires, forging weapons of various types. Yani noticed spears, swords, crossbows and even some stun guns, issued only to the town militia forces.

"To be used when all the Ells have gone," said the Panther, "for this man." Krask's huge physique filled the screen. He stood overseeing the work, then started shouting for more metal to be poured. "That is the leader, a power-mad dictator-in-waiting."

"He keeps prisoners too, various scientists and one very special one, an Ell lady, I believe. He broadcasts a vibration that interferes with the Ell spy-bees and so keeps his preparations secret."

"Mother..." Yani whispered. He coughed awkwardly, hoping this rather eccentric soldier had not heard him, then asked, "where is that mountain exactly, do you know?" If he could find the mountain, he could find his mother. This soldier was becoming more interesting by the minute.

"That I do not know, other than that it is in the Pyrenees. But listen to me, will you take up the role of Earth Lord for the rest of your life? Scotch this nest of scorpions and all like it? Rule and control this world so that mankind is kept on righteous paths? Exercise power as it should be used?"

The General's eyes shone with fervour, his voice was clear and fierce, like a battle cry. Yani sighed and shook his head.

"For four hundred years the Ells have ruled this planet and some still question whether or not this was right. You are suggesting that I should now take absolute control?"

Yani felt the stirrings of ambition and the appetite for power. However he had enough wisdom to see where it could lead him.

"No thank you, sir," he said, "only enough power to get the job done – and all decisions to be agreed with the World Council. However, tell me where that mountain is!"

The General shook his head. "I only know it lies in the central Pyrenees, I was given the information to tempt you, but I see that you are already strong enough to resist." He sighed. "So be it. A young man should develop a firm character. Your path leads that way, to the temple," and he pointed towards a hill someway off, "and I go in the other direction. I salute you!" and he marched off.

It took Yani longer than he expected to reach the hill and, lacking any advice to the contrary, he decided to climb to the top where there was some sort of temple. Approaching it, he could see that it consisted of a series of marble pillars supporting a circular domed roof. Open to the winds, it had an aura of great tranquillity. Yani walked into the centre and sat down on a white rectangular bench. Lifesized carvings of men and women, one on each pillar, faced inwards, each one conveying a sense of wisdom as deep as time. Yani felt they were all looking at him intently and he wished that they could speak.

"Oh, but we can," said a voice inside his head, "Look around you, beyond the temple."

Somehow not surprised, Yani stood up and walked round the temple. Circled by a low ground mist, it now seemed to float on air.

Out and beyond, there stretched a vast panorama of mountains, islands and ocean, all crystal clear under the sun. Yani felt he could have counted the grains of sand on the distant beaches had he wished. He could see the great waves surge and retreat, leaving filigrees of spume to dry in the sun. From far off he heard the cry of gulls amid the steady thunder from the shore.

Among the mountains, blue on the horizon, he saw eagles wheeling and turning as they searched for food. The whole world exuded a timeless beauty, and Yani's heart sang with joy.

"Timeless it is, Yani, for here you stand for a moment outside time, in a higher realm that is not entirely of this world. You have come here from the Tower of Temptation but to the Earth you must soon return.

"Lie down on the bench, close your eyes and relax. We will give you such guidance as we can. You will find a flagon of water beneath the bench. Drink from it, then rest."

Yani bent down, found the flagon and took a long draught of the sweetest water he had ever tasted. Infused with herbs and heather it was utterly refreshing. A gentle lassitude spread through his limbs and he lay down and closed his eyes. He continued to wonder about the figures in the pillars and wasn't surprised when they continued to speak in his mind.

"We are the Elders. We represent the best aspirations of life. This Temple is not a physical place; it exists only in the realm of thought and you have come here in your mind. Now, have you been told that everything you think of as solid material, is in fact made of energy? Look at this!"

Floating in space Yani saw a dim fuzzy sun. He looked out from this solar system into a great gulf to see distant twinkling stars. "Where is the Earth?" he wondered.

There was gentle laughter. "You are looking inside a grain of sand and in a different dimension of time. In Earth terms, time, at the place you see, has virtually stopped. Now, come back to the Temple." Yani opened his eyes and found it was night.

"Look outside!" and he rose, walked to the edge of the floor and stood between two pillars. Night had fallen. The velvet-black sky blazed with stars. Yani gazed in wonder at the vast spectacle, trying to understand why all this, and the universe of atoms he had just seen, were so similar.

"As above, so below," as the sages of old taught. Everything, from the smallest to the largest, exists in the web of creation. Now you have seen for yourself the structure of everything, you will understand better. What you see as solid matter is not solid at all. Nothing from the very large, like the universe, to the very small, like the structure of atoms, is "solid" in the way people think. That is an illusion created by energy, and energy comes from emotion powered by thought.

"Focussed thought and emotion produce vibrations which affect the very structure of things. The Ells` brains generate much stronger vibrations than humans, giving them the ability to alter matter. Vibrations can be constructive, destructive or neutral in their effect. Even the weak vibrations produced by humans have effects. Even for them, thoughts influence events. With your special abilities you must take extra care to guard against negative thoughts."

"That's how it worked," Yani thought, remembering the old broom handle channelling his anger. He returned to the bench and lay down again.

"Only four Ells remain on Earth and soon they too will depart. Humankind must evolve unaided. However, there are still some renegades with stolen Ell technology and some even have Ell genes, so a few half-Ells should remain behind to counter them."

"The Guardians!" Yani exclaimed.

"Are you prepared to become a Guardian?"

"Oh yes!"

"To become a Guardian, you must spend time learning different skills. Practice meditation, morning and evening. Leave the search for Elaire to your grandparents"

"But I must help them find Mother," cried the boy.

"You should wait until you are fully trained or you could make matters worse." Yani bit his lip and frowned, but the voice continued. "Later you will receive a special instrument to help you: use it wisely.

"Now you must return to your world. We will give you a scroll and a package for Arlinda. Remember that half of you is human, so sometimes you may fail the Ell`s high standards, but never give up and never despair! You have to come to terms with your dual heritage. Above all, be yourself. Listen to your spirit. Yani, farewell."

As if waking from a dream, Yani found himself at the top of the staircase which, reluctantly, he started to descend. This time no invitations were extended but one or two individuals called to him: "Remember me if we meet again!"

Eventually he reached the ground hall. There, awaiting him, was another meal, a package and a rolled parchment with a label which said "For the Lady Arlinda, who will be waiting for you in the morning." Suddenly ravenous, Yani demolished everything on the table, then lay down on the couch and fell asleep.

As he dreamt, a figure came to him. It shone with light so he could not see its face, but he knew that the light was love. It laid a tiny jewel on his forehead, saying, "In this Jewel are the seven colours of the Rainbow, each with its own seed of wisdom. Like all seeds these need time to grow. How they develop will depend on the care and nourishment you give them by meditation. Each has its own particular aspect, its own special music—and true music is the language of the Ells, a gift from the Creator."

More was said which Yani did not remember till later. The brightness faded, the word "Farewell" rang like a bell, diminishing...diminishing...and a great sense of separation fell upon him like a black night: now he was truly on his own. The Jewel dissolved into him, as a seed is accepted by the earth.

Yani woke with morning light pouring in through the high windows. He hurried outside to find a perfectly normal path leading down to where Arlinda was walking up and down on the turf. The mist had gone, the air was fresh and sunlight sparkled on the dew.

"It`s only been two days," said Yani.

"Ha! You were there for thirty days. I told you it was a strange place. Anyhow, look how you've grown. You're almost as tall as me," laughed his grandmother, giving him a welcoming hug then, holding him at arm's length, she looked into his face. He had changed, leaner and taller certainly, and the boyishness had firmed into early manhood. Here stood a determined youngster, returning her gaze from a pair of steady eyes, as fathomless and blue as the ocean.

"I can see you did well," she added, "But I'll ask no questions. You may tell me as little or as much as you wish, for now you are a young man with a man`s voice."

Yani flushed slightly, then remembered to hand over the scroll of parchment and the package.

"Very medieval," Arlinda remarked, breaking the wax seal. She frowned as she read the scroll, then paced round the bubble flyer several times."Hmm," she said, "Hmm."

Yani looked at her anxiously, for Arlinda was obviously disconcerted, then, giving a deep sigh, she said; "I believe that you've already been told something about this?" and Yani told her what the Elders had said.

"No travelling the star trails with the Ells, little life among your own kindred – what did you say?"

"That I would become a Guardian," said Yani, "but Mother must be found."

CHAPTER SEVEN

1

Old Memories

For a while on the return trip Arlinda seemed deep in thought, then she roused herself. "Yani, my dear, there is something else the Elders recommend. It will be difficult for you to cope with at your age, but I must be guided by them."

"What is it?" Yani asked in his new deep voice, trying to sound as serious and grown up as he could.

"When we first came here—the Intervention—there were a few brave men who, knowing what we intended to do, offered their lives' memories to us. They asked if Ell technology could copy the complete memories of a person and transfer it to others. It's only the memories of their ego, not their soul which has of course gone elsewhere."

"Why did they suggest this?"

"Those far sighted people came to us and said, 'In the future there will be diehards among our people who will oppose you. They will argue that the Intervention was not necessary. Let them experience our lives and that will convince them.'

"We developed a method to do this, but few survived the operation. We took care only to perform it when their natural lives were nearing their end, but old people can have a strong will to live as long as possible, so it was a noble sacrifice."

"What's this to do with me?"

"I have been given this disc containing the memory of one of those special men. The Elders want you to have his memory as soon as possible. It's far more overpowering than watching a story on a screen or in virtual reality. In twelve hours you will dream the entire life experience of someone else. It is such a vivid experience that you will need weeks to recover. Furthermore, the memories will remain with you for ever."

Yani frowned. "The Elders have recommended this for me now?"

"For all who would be Guardians, but you are the youngest. We have discs selected for your friends and had intended to do this next year."

Yani thought back to those wise faces on the pillars and the joy and peace they had conveyed. Dangerous or not...

"Grandma, we must trust them."

Arlinda bit her lip but said nothing. She glanced at Yani quickly but saw no uncertainty clouding his clean-cut features. "Oh my darling boy," she thought, "pitchforked into real life before he's had time to grow up properly."

Next morning, back in Altania, Arlinda saw Dr Macgregor and asked him to prepare a memory induction session for the five students in three days time. He bristled with indignation. "But the lad's just recovering from the Tower! This could unsettle him completely. The others have had months to settle. Are you sure of this?"

"Sure? No, but the Elders are."

Macgregor shook his head and went off to make the preparations, muttering under his breath about running before walking.

Arlinda offered each of them the chance to opt out. No one took it.

"Each of you will have a different memory implant. Afterwards you will go to a quiet island where you can recover at your own pace."

"Please explain more so that we can understand, why this process was necessary?" Turias asked.

"You can't deal with problems unless you understand what causes them, especially when they are political or religious. This will give you an understanding you could not get any other way."

"I can see it helping us to spot any of the old problems coming back," Lucy said, "so let's do it," and she glanced at her brother, who looked worried.

Turias said, "Won't it be like having someone else inside your head. I like to be in control of myself—"

"And others," Pasco muttered.

Turias ignored him. "I don't like the idea but, if the Elders recommend it, I'll accept."

Ragore was the least concerned. "It will be interesting," he said.

"That I can promise you," Arlinda remarked.

Yani looked round the room where he was about to experience another world in another time. He saw a comfortable bed with a large helmet set.

"What do I do?" he asked Dr Macgregor.

"Lie down on the bed, put on the helmet and I will give you an injection. I've already dealt with the others. You will be lightly sedated and feel at peace before we start the process. Just try and relax."

For the next twelve hours Arlinda and Macgregor watched the students for any signs of distress. Arlinda remembered her own induction, all the memories of a twentieth century lady doctor still lived in her mind, but it was the emotional shockwave of being someone else that worried her now. It had taken her several weeks to come to terms with the duality of her memory. She paid great attention to Yani—would this inexperienced youngster be able to cope?

By late evening the process was finished and Arlinda gently removed the helmet and, full of trepidation, examined Yani's face. He seemed to be sleeping peacefully, his golden hair framing the face she had come to know so well—but who lurked behind it now? Was it her dear grandson, so keen to rescue his mother, or was it a man of the past, whose strong personality would overpower a youngster not yet fully developed?

Hours passed, midnight approached and still he slept. Would he ever waken, or would he remain in some sort of coma? Trembling now with nervous exhaustion, Arlinda missed the flicker of Yani's eyelids. Suddenly his blue eyes were looking into hers. She clutched his hand. Would he know her?

A deep voice demanded, "Where am I?"

Arlinda sighed, this was not her Yani. She let go his hand and stood up. She tried to speak with reassurance. "You're in the garden city of Altania, and your name is Yani. You've been through—"

"I know who I am, and my name is certainly not Yani, but who are you? Also I demand to know what the Ells are doing about things. The whole planet is in danger. I risked my life to help them and some even called me traitor for it. Me, Guy Sinclair, a traitor!"

"Come outside," Arlinda said, "and see where you are." Her legs trembled, but she kept her head high and led the way to a balcony overlooking the gardens.

Yani strode after her then stopped abruptly. "Where is this place? I've never seen it before—but …but I recognize that mountain behind. Where have all these buildings come from?"

"I told you, this is Altania, garden city of the Ells."

Yani said nothing as he took in the symmetry of the layout and the elegance of the buildings. Arlinda had a moment to think how she might disperse the shadow on Yani's mind.

She turned and picked up a hand mirror. "Look into this," she said.

Yani's head turned slowly. Ignoring the mirror, he stared deep into Arlinda's eyes. "This is amazing," he said, "how has all this come about. I was here, or near here, only recently, to have my memory copied. These towers were not here."

"Yes indeed," Arlinda humoured him, "but please look in the mirror."

At last Yani looked at his reflection. Staring wide-eyed, slowly he raised his hands to his face, pushing at his cheeks, running fingers through his hair. He shuddered violently, swung round and grasped the wrought-iron railing. He pulled against it, trying to tear it from the brickwork. Sobs shook his body then he gave a terrible cry of despair, "Gone, gone, Elizabeth, my family, all gone."

He fell to the ground and rolled up into a ball, head pressed against his knees. Arlinda knelt and laid her hand on his shoulder. "Come, lie down and rest for a little while. You are Yani, and you`ve been dreaming about someone who lived long ago. Try to remember your real life."

Silently, Yani allowed her to lead him back to the couch where he lay down quietly and closed his eyes.

Arlinda went to see Macgregor. "How are the others," she enquired. "Yani`s very confused."

"Not surprising, I said he was too young. The others are very quiet but at least they know who they are. It took us weeks to return to normal."

"Their company will be the best thing for Yani. He can`t have forgotten his friends altogether. We`ll take them off to the islands now, no point in wasting time."

From high up, the group of islands resembled jewels lying on an aquamarine cloth. As they descended, the students made out long thatched buildings, sheltered by palm trees. The flier landed on grass beside a beach of coral sand and the students were welcomed by the wash of waves on the shore and the soft rustle of wind in the palms.

"Everything is arranged," Arlinda said. "You must relax, swim, sail, make music and, above all, talk about your new memories. This is a healing time. Dr Macgregor will be available in the hotel`s main building and can join you in the evenings when you wish. You each have your own hut and there are no other guests. Enjoy yourselves and I shall return in a few weeks."

She looked anxiously at Yani, who had not spoken a word. He continued to look at everything around him as if he were in a dream.

Turias saw Arlinda`s fear. "Don`t worry," he said, "we`ll look after him. It`ll just take him longer to surface." He turned to Yani. "Come on, my young friend, and we`ll have a look at this place where we`re going to stay. I`ll carry your case for you, not that we`ll need much in the way of clothes here"

Unprotesting, Yani allowed himself to be led off to his hut. Lucy, Pasco and Ragore followed behind.

"Look," Ragore said, standing outside Yani's hut, "it's going to be a fabulous sunset. Let's just sit down and watch it. We can unpack later."

"Yani, sit beside me," Lucy coaxed him, and for the next ten minutes they all watched the rapid sunset of the tropics. Little lights sprang up among the huts and someone started a fire in the barbecue pit.

"Smell that," Ragore said, "we haven't eaten for a lifetime, or was it only yesterday?" Even Yani started to show some interest and joined in the feast that followed.

"He's still not spoken," Lucy murmured to Turias, whose teak-like face maintained a reassuring calmness. "He will," he replied, "just give him time."

Next morning Macgregor encouraged them to go windsurfing, "It'll force you to concentrate on immediate things, like staying alive!" he said. "I know you are overwhelmed by these memories of another time, but your life is here and now. We'll keep the evenings for talking and questions."

Turias glanced at Yani. "You've slept well," he said. "would you like to try this wind surfing?"

"I used to be very good at it," Yani replied in a distant tone.

Ragore stared at Yani. "But—"

"Quiet, Ragore," Lucy stopped him. "It's his new memory remembering."

Two hours later, Ragore, coughing seawater out of his chest, watched Yani skimming about on his board like a seagull on the wing. "Look at that," he spluttered, "his new memory must be working well. He's never been on these things before."

"It's still working too well," Pasco said, as he passed. "Come on Ragore, balance yourself like Yani, or whoever he thinks he is."

Later, as evening again stained the sky, the tired four sat in a circle on the sand. No one seemed to want to speak first, but finally Lucy said, "Come on, we've got to talk about it." She looked at Yani. "Remember the first time you saw us, covered with nets at our camp fire?"

Yani gazed into the distance, frowning, then slowly his head nodded. "I remember," he said, his voice sounding stronger. "Yes, I remember chasing those bandits, didn't they look silly wrapped up in their own nets."

Suddenly he jumped to his feet, eyes wide open. "I am Yani," he cried, "Yan t'Ell, grandson of Zandor... what a dream I've had. It was a strange world, good and bad, and—." He stopped and looked round. "Of course you've all been there too, only I couldn't wake up. Oh I'm so sorry, I've caused you worry, I'm an idiot."

Lucy threw her arms around him. "No you're not, you were just too young and whoever it was overpowered you for a while."

"He also turned you into a better windsurfer than me, than any of us, and I wasn't pleased," Ragore interrupted, and then they all laughed; they had their friend back.

"It was the way life was then that I find so difficult to understand," Pasco said. "I mean why did people behave so stupidly, fighting over old traditions, grabbing for more of everything?"

"And life was so unfair for many people," Lucy replied, then suddenly the dam broke and they all started talking at once about the rights and wrongs of the old world.

Yani spoke least but, as they were all growing tired, finally contributed.

"Here we are, picking up ancient troubles and arguing them again. If we are not careful we'll give them fresh life. Surely what matters is to find out how the Ells changed things around."

"You're right," Turias said. "Dr Macgregor can show us what they did. He told me he has these holographic discs with him if we want to see them."

Ragore yawned, "Well not tonight. I'm going to dream of those recipes I remember from the old days."

"Trust Arlinda to give you the memory of one of the great chefs," Lucy said. "I got that of a doctor in the World Health Organization. It was pretty hellish, I can tell you. Anyway, I`m off to sleep."

Yani woke early from recurring dreams of Sinclair`s life. "But I`m me, Yani," he told himself. "That was long ago. All these people are gone. The lovely Elizabeth, his children, his grandchildren…all gone."

He walked out and down to the beach A pink dawn lit the calm sea and he noticed a large figure sitting at the water`s edge. Turias looked round.

"So you didn`t sleep too well either?" he asked.

Yani shook his head. "I woke and wondered who I am. It all seemed so real—."

"It was real, once, but everything`s much better now." Turias got to his feet and put his large hand on Yani`s shoulder. "What we need now is more exercise and real life excitement. Tire ourselves out, then we`ll sleep better tonight."

Gradually, days of sea and sun, with evenings spent sharing memories, healed the invasion of their minds. Macgregor played discs showing the work of the Ells during the early years of the Intervention. They saw satellites spreading a gigantic gas blanket in space to shield the poles from their summer sunshine. They saw the recovery of huge areas of rain forest and deserts turned to green savannah lands, which became new homes for those who had been dispossessed.

That evening Macgregor joined them on the beach. "Now you have experienced what this world was like before the Intervention I suppose you have some questions."

"Only about a thousand or so," Turias replied. "Could you tell me what happened to all the people? What about all the chasing after material things, the greed, the violence, etc?"

"We had to make many changes but I`m not going to bore you with a long list of these tonight—you can watch these on the discs later—but I will tell you a story."

"I like stories," Lucy said, "They remind me of my childhood."

Macgregor smiled. "This is not a story for children. Zelton first told it to the United Nations in one of his sessions there. See what you make of it.....

"Once when time and the world were young there was a mountain, the largest there has ever been. Its northern slopes lay in the cool lands where winter winds brought ice and snow, but its southern valleys knew no such chills. They basked in hot sunshine and their shores were washed by warm seas.

"The mountain peak, the highest there has ever been, glittered with snow all year round, and glaciers graced its upper slopes with their majestic presence. Halfway down a great plateau encircled the entire mountain. Here, below the glaciers, lakes spread to nestle among the gentler hills and wooded slopes. From each lake a river sprang so that, on all sides of the great mountain, long steep valleys were carved as the waters hurried down to the surrounding seas.

"The people living in these valleys were quite cut-off from neighbouring communities, and remained in ignorance of their very existence. Each of these communities flourished and grew over many centuries but few attempts were made to explore beyond their fertile valleys. None of those who sought to do so ever returned. Each community had a different view of the great mountain's peak. When it was not wrapped in cloud it presented an entirely different aspect to those who viewed it from the north, south, east and west, to take but four examples.

"The occasional glimpses of the glittering peak inspired thoughts of heaven among the religious leaders in each community. So perfect, so unworldly did this vision seem, that it was adopted by all the different communities as their belief of heaven. Remember, of course, that no two views were the same. The dwellers in the eastern valleys saw a peak that shone brightest in the morning sun while those in the west accepted evening as the hour of worship.

"Any chance meeting with dwellers from another valley, such as occasionally took place among fishing boats often led to arguments as to the nature of heaven and the local priests used this as a good reason to despise neighbours. Indeed, they saw this as a threat to their power and influence; intermingling with other communities was universally forbidden.

"Any curious person who climbed up the long valleys and discovered the great plateau lands, was welcomed back by execution for blasphemy. Aware of this custom, those who went away, stayed away. They found fellow adventurers from other communities and also a much wider and more accurate comprehension of their world. First villages, then towns and cities grew over the centuries, and a civilisation evolved based on tolerance and understanding.

"Keen to recruit greater numbers to the plateau, but aware of the closed minds of the valley dwellers, attempts to enlighten them were limited to sending messages from the heights by way of flashing lights or smoking fires. This did arouse curiosity, much to the fury of the priests, who sought to tighten their grip by punishing any who dared to ask questions about the cause of such phenomenon."

Lucy looked hard at Dr. Macgregor. "You want us to work out the meaning behind this story?"

"Of course."

"Well I think you`re trying to show us how divided people were by narrow mindedness."

Pasco agreed with Lucy but Yani said "Surely it`s more than that. Is it not a picture of how Earth was? We can see that the Creator was given different names by different religions and this led to terrible wars and cruelty, but why should the Creator care what name people give him?"

Turias nodded, adding "or which path they take to climb the mountain."

"Also," Yani added, "it shows that you can only climb one path at a time."

"And respect the paths others choose," Lucy said.

Macgregor looked round at the earnest young faces, smiled and wished them goodnight. He left them to the waves and the stars.

By the time to return to Altania came, the students all carried an invaluable and powerful new weapon—a deeper understanding of the past.

CHAPTER EIGHT

Estella.

Estella watched the four male students from her solitary seat by the far window. She had not seen them around for some time and wondered where they had been. Her father wished her to ensnare one of them; it promised to be the easiest part of her duties down here—provided they didn't disappear again.

The question was—which one? Turias towered over the others, but he seemed too serious and already set in his ways. Pasco's sister kept careful watch on her brother and, while Ragore would be easy to conquer, Estella liked a challenge.

Yani, although younger, intrigued her with his golden hair and brilliant eyes. He had been away for two months and returned changed. He had grown taller, his shoulders had broadened and now he carried himself with a sense of purpose. The puzzled, touchy youth had vanished and, while anger still smouldered inside, it was well hidden. Estella wondered what had happened to change him so quickly. Now she would have a real challenge on her hands.

Although attending different classes, Estella was known to be a hard working girl who kept her own company. With hair like midnight, eyes green as the sea and a sweet, heart-shaped face, Estella had not gone unnoticed by Ragore, who had made several attempts to get to know her better. Politely, she had kept him at a distance till he had decided to seek easier game.

"Come sailing with us on Saturday, Yani," Pasco urged. "Its just Lucy and me and we need fresh air after this week's class work."

"I know little about sailing dinghies, Sinclair preferred wind surfing."

"Similar principle, but Lucy`s experienced and she`ll teach you."

"I thought you grew up in Andorra. How did she learn—"

"To sail there? No, an uncle lived down on the coast and we spent holidays with him."

Yani`s attention had drifted. "Who`s that girl looking at us?" he asked Pasco. "Dark hair and very pretty."

"Oh, so you`ve noticed! Ragore tried to ask her out but she"s very studious, works all the time."

"Really? Ragore asked her out?"

"Interested are we?" Pasco teased, then added more seriously, "careful with that one, she'll break your heart.... to be honest I don't trust her."

"You don't trust her? Come on Pasco!" Yani laughed. Pasco just shrugged, he was not too concerned as Yani had never shown any interest in girls in a romantic sense. Since they had returned from the island, Yani just seemed in a hurry to get through the course as fast as possible; mostly work and little play.

"Come on then, introduce me, maybe she'll come sailing too?" Yani said. "Do it now while Ragore beats Turias at chess."

"It`s good to be able to beat him at something," Ragore muttered, deep in thought.

The students` dining room was nearly empty when Pasco led Yani over to where Estella sat, engrossed in an old volume.

"Estella, er, sorry to interrupt you, but my good friend Yani here wanted to be introduced."

"Hello,"she said, glancing up from her book.

"Hello, Estella. What are you reading?" Yani asked. He produced a dazzling smile and sat down opposite her. Estella put her book down slowly, trying to maintain some poise.

"It's something I love, a book about the old poets." She raised an eyebrow in challenge, surely he knew nothing about historical poetry?

"Who`s your favourite? I like Chesterton myself." Yani said, genuinely interested and, thanking Sinclair`s memory, he quoted;
"You never loved your friends, my friends, as I have loved my foes."

Estella was startled. Had he read her intentions so quickly?

"That`s a strange choice, I prefer "Lepanto," the story of a great battle, remember
"Dim drums throbbing, in the hills half heard...."

"Really? War, an unusual subject for a girl," and, to Pasco`s disgust, the two started to look up poems and quote favourite lines. Lucy came in and Pasco waved her over. Yani rose and greeted her as she joined them. Estella watched the interaction between the three as they made plans to go sailing. She found herself warming to them all, especially Yani; imagine him knowing Chesterton.

"Estella," Yani turned his sapphire eyes on her once again, "what are you doing on Saturday afternoon?"

"Oh, I'm not sure…" she frowned.

"Would you like to come sailing with us?" Yani asked. She looked at the three of them, and smiled.

"Yes, that would be lovely, but I know little about it."

Lucy sat down beside Estella and started to tell her all about their boat. Pasco put his hand on Yani's arm and drew him a little away from the girls.

"A word of warning, dear chap," he ventured.

Yani shook his head. "Here we go, life according to Pasco, is it?"

"Oh come on, I mean Chesterton? How did you manage to pull that one?"

"Easy, Sinclair`s memory—he loved poetry. You need to read more, Pasco, poetry`s great." But all the time Pasco noticed Yani was watching Estella, a grin all over his face. Yani was smitten and Pasco was not happy about this, not happy at all.

A violent squall struck the dinghy, which heeled over sharply. Estella shrieked as she threw herself against Yani, watching with terrified fascination as the gunnels below them kissed the water. Lucy swung the bow round to point downwind, just after a curling wave had chucked a sheet of white foam over them.

"We've tacked upwind long enough," she called. "Now we'll really move!"

"But the wind's gone," Estella remarked a moment later and Pasco, sitting forward, laughed.

"Oh no it hasn't, we're just travelling with it instead of fighting it, as we have been all day. Look at the shore!"

In the eerie calm of sailing downwind, both Yani and Estella peered landwards. Over the lacy flutterings of the breakers on the rocks, they could see the land slipping past at an amazing rate. They were skimming the waves, keeping pace with them, driven by the wind's power on the straining sails.

Reluctant to release Estella's grip on him, and enjoying the feel of her salt-wet cheek on his, Yani rejoiced. At sea, land-bound troubles shrank from view; all that mattered was pitting yourself against the elements and staying alive in the sun, wind and waves. Having a girl like Estella snuggled beside him woke strange feelings inside. Life coursed through him; the water might not drown him, but happiness might.

"At this speed we could sail right on to Bellaporto, eat there and take a flyer back to Altania. The port is a fun place at weekends. The flamenco is fantastic."

Yani looked at Estella, and raised a questioning eyebrow. "I've never had time off since I came here," she said sadly.

"That's crazy!" Lucy cried, "why ever not?"

"It's just that Father needs me to learn so much so quickly and—"

"Well, a night off now and then will freshen your mind," Pasco chipped in, feeling slightly uncomfortable about his suspicions. The poor girl had an ogre for a father, most un-Ell like. No wonder she had been standoffish.

As they tied the dinghy up an hour later, Yani asked why they didn't sail back through the night."Against this gale? No, we'll fetch her when there's a good east breeze."

The glamour of the port entranced them, the lights of little restaurants lined the waterfront, their various appetizing aromas mingling with the sound of guitars and voices singing.

They chose a Basque restaurant, hoping for good Pyrenean food to satisfy a whole day's hunger, and Estella, Lucy and Pasco reminisced about the mountains. Yani said little, being happy to sit and watch Estella chatting. Her eyes, emerald bright, sparkled as laughter lit her heart shaped face. "This is the most fun I've had in years," she said. "You are all so happy together."

"But this is normal, we are all friends," Lucy replied.

"Normal for you, but not for me; I have to work so hard."

"Well you've got friends now," Yani said, grasping her hand. Her heart leaped and she squeezed back. After all, doing what her father ordered for once went along with what her heart wanted.

"Now listen Estella," Yani said, "this nonsense of non-stop work must cease. From now on you must spend your evenings with us. Ragore is an expert on where to go and when money's short we go to the beach, listen to the waves, count the stars and work out what life is all about."

Her eyes grew misty. "I could join you?" and she looked at the others.

"Of course you can."

She subdued the feeling that she would betray their trust, jumped to her feet and laughed, "Come on Yani, let's dance."

As she taught him one or two dance steps Yani found himself gazing into the green pools of her eyes, inhaling her perfume and all sorts of yearnings woke in his heart. This was a new kind of friendship; the village girls in Polonia had despised and tormented him. Estella was warm and welcoming and now she sparkled with life.

During the next few weeks Estella found herself accepted as one of this happy group. Lucy in particular made a special effort to befriend her, though it was Yani who spent all the time he could with her.

Very late one evening, when Yani had been kept back by Dr Macgregor to complete a complicated exercise, it was Lucy who walked Estella back to her room. It was quiet in the grounds, many rooms were cloaked in darkness, the students within asleep.

Lucy took a deep breath. This would be stepping beyond her normal chat, and she didn`t want to upset Estella. "You and Yani seem to be quite serious?"she hedged.

Estella glanced at her. "Has Yani said anything about me?"she asked, unable to keep her mouth from smiling. Her heart beat a little faster. "Well, has he?" she added as Lucy didn`t responded at once.

"Oh he doesn`t need to, his eyes say it all when he looks at you," Lucy teased. "You know you are the envy of all the girl students here."

"I am very fond of him," Estella said after a thoughtful silence.

"Fond—is that all, are you sure?" Lucy took Estella`s hand in a gentle grip. "Estella, I don`t want you to get hurt. You know he has some sort of personal quest, something dangerous, that he is determined to do, don`t you?"

Estella drew a quick breath. "Dangerous, surely not. I`ve always felt there was something lurking in his mind, but it could take him into danger?"

"Perhaps you should ask him."

"Yes, Lucy, you`re right. I will."

Lucy sighed and released Estella`s hand. "You aren`t the first to fall for him, you know, but the first in whom he has shown any interest. He`s become like a brother to me but even I can see his attraction—these amazing eyes and the way he gives all his attention when he`s talking to you. He will be very difficult to resist; Estella be careful."

No more was said till they reached Estella`s door. "Lucy, I do appreciate your warning. I know he seems about sixteen, and I`m only two years older but I think it`s really quite serious for Yani and for me. Neither of us have felt like this before."

"Well be extra careful, don't get carried away."

Her father's dictates sprang into Estella's mind. Lucy would be horrified. She blushed and turned away. "Yes, Lucy, I understand. Goodnight," and with conflicting loyalties boiling in her mind, she closed the door, putting an end to any further conversation.

She went to the window and pressed her forehead against the cool glass. All her life her father and Zenia had insisted on a strong sense of duty to their cause—but was it really her cause? These young half Ells didn't seem so dreadful, in fact they were the nicest people she had met. Eighteen years of conditioning were hard to combat but her father's instructions rang in her head.

Oh this was hopeless, which way should she turn? She peered out into the night.

Perhaps Yani would still visit her, then she checked the time and the faint hope died. It was too late.

A week later a favourable easterly wind brought the four sailors back to Bellaporto to retrieve their little craft. The return sail was straightforward and later Yani walked Estella back to her room.

"Come in," she invited, "and explain what's bothering you. Despite all our fun I sense that, deep down, something is nagging at you."

Yani followed her inside, sighed, and said, "It's my mother. She's a prisoner somewhere and I don't know where or how. She's an Ell and to keep an Ell against their will should not be possible."

Estella stared at Yani as she realized whose son he was— her father's prisoner. She drew a deep breath, and fought to keep her face sympathetic.

Yani's eyes darkened with pain as, taking her silence for sympathy, he told her about a small boy, camping with his parents, wandering off with a friend for a few hours and returning to utter devastation, his shelter and parents gone and only his dog left, and then years of loneliness.

Estella forced herself to remember her father's words. "In war," he had told her, "you can't be squeamish. The Ells took over our planet and imposed their soft ways on us. We are the last hope of Earth's true heritage and we must be prepared to do anything to restore it. Personal feelings don't count!"

"So what do you want to do, Yani?" she asked.

"Do? What do I—why go and find her of course! My mother's in the hands of goodness knows who or where. She whispered to me in my dreams for ten years—she needs me and I must go. I believe she is somewhere in the central Pyrenees, in a cave, but how I'll find her I don't know, but I'll die trying."

Estella thought quickly. Perhaps there was a way that she could get him back later. Her father always wanted Ell blood on his side. If he captured Yani and could convince him that the Ells had been wrong.....If he was kept separate from his mother, didn't learn that Krask was her captor.....

"Yani" Estella said quietly, "Listen. I come from the central Pyrenees and I know a man who knows more about caves than anyone. I could write to him and ask him to help you. He lives halfway between Taca and Pilgrims' Gap near a big waterfall, easy to find."

"That would be fantastic, a tremendous help, oh please do," and Yani picked her up and hugged her, then suddenly he was kissing her and everything changed. This girl brought him alive as never before. He would save her from this ogre of a father. Once their studies were complete they could marry and be together forever. After all he was sixteen, at least in human terms, and surely that was old enough to start making important decisions.

Later, after Yani had left, Estella wrote a letter to Pedro Domingues. Her father had been emphatic about security.

"Letters are the safest communication for us. Anything electronic can be monitored. It's best they don't know you are my daughter, so route everything through Pedro."

88

She fought down the knowledge that she was betraying her new friends and told herself that she was doing the best thing for Yani. Krask would show him the error of his ways and afterwards Yani would be hers, permanently. They would marry and live at Eagleskeep; her father would be delighted.

CHAPTER NINE

Alone

No positive news had yet come from Zandor, still searching up in the central Pyrenees. The Panther's remarks to Yani about Elaire's whereabouts had been taken very seriously.

Meanwhile the July vacation couldn't come quickly enough for Yani. Lucy planned to visit a friend in the Hebrides while Turias, Pasco and Ragore had organized a sail in the Mediterranean that would take about three weeks. They expected Yani to go with them and Arlinda assumed that he would. At the last moment Yani, feeling guilty, said he had decided not to go with them.

"But it will be a great adventure!" enthused Pasco.

Ragore just smiled, "Perhaps he has something better to do. Remember the gorgeous Estella!"

"Have a great trip, see you when you get back!" he called as they left. Turias was last out the door. He looked searchingly at Yani and shook his head. "You've been very jumpy of late. Are you sure you'll be all right?"

Yani took a deep breath, better for his friends if they didn't know what he had in mind; they would want to come with him if they guessed.

"I'll be fine," he said. "I hope you get good weather."

Yani didn't want to drag them into danger; after all, it was his mother, so he should be the one to take any risks that might arise.

Also he said nothing to Arlinda, allowing her to assume that he was joining his friends on their sailing expedition. He told his conscience that he was saving her worry and, when his trip discovered where his mother actually was, everyone would be delighted.

The day of departure finally arrived. Yani threw some clothes into his rucksack and left for the tube station. He took a ticket to Taca, via Madrid and, going down in the escalator, felt he was setting out on a great mission. At last he was going to do something about finding his mother. Zandor had spent months around the Pyrenees and discovered nothing so far. This man Pedro might well be able to pinpoint caves no one else knew about.

Yani stepped into the carriage and found a row of twenty double seats, one behind the other, placed down the centre passage. As soon as he sat down, a screen lit up on the back of the seat in front of him.

"Welcome! Please fasten your seat belt and do not undo it until the tube is stationary at Madrid. Once cruising speed has been reached, the seats will swivel round to support you against the fierce deceleration. Departure in one minute!"

The doors closed and a strong and increasing force pushed Yani back into his chair. This continued for a few minutes, then ceased. Had they stopped? There was little sensation of movement, just the occasional tremor and Yani took a deep breath; he was moving towards his mother at tremendous speed.

His chair began to turn round and again the screen lit up. "Arrival in Madrid in six minutes, deceleration in one minute." Yani couldn't believe it. They had just started a few minutes ago and they had covered hundreds of kilometres already!

When they stopped at Madrid, the seats swivelled round again and all other passengers left, except for one man sitting at the front. Yani sat deep in thought, recalling the images of Elaire he had seen in Altania. These had revived his childhood memories. Why would someone be so wicked as to separate her from him all these years ago? Yani clenched his fists in a reflex action from his "village years." Four months with the peaceful Ells had not eliminated his anger; he was now sixteen in human terms, he had been to the Tower and his Ell abilities were growing. Absorbed in his memories, he barely noticed that the carriage had set off again, and they were decelerating for Taca before he started thinking about his immediate needs.

As the carriage stopped, the passenger in front of him stood up and, turning round, apologized for not speaking earlier.

"The seating arrangement hardly helps conversation," he said. "May I introduce myself—my name is Salvador Allendez. I take it you`ve come up to the mountains for some decent air?"

"And I am Yan t` Ell, but everyone calls me Yani," Yani replied, examining the stranger carefully.

Salvador, a grey haired man of medium build, returned Yani`s scrutiny from a pair of friendly, hazel eyes. He led Yani over to the lift and waved him in. "Welcome to the old town of Taca!"

He continued to talk as they ascended to street level and Yani found it difficult to get a word in. Finally he realized that Salvador was asking if he could be of any assistance.

"There is one thing," Yani said, "I need to hire a horse for about a month so if you…"

"A horse? Nothing easier. Esteban is a very reliable chap with extra reliable horses," he laughed. "Come, they are just nearby. Lots of people up from Madrid in the summer hire from him as they need to shake off city life now and then."

Yani found himself being borne along on this tide of goodwill, which didn't stop even when they reached the stables.

"Senor Esteban!" Salvador called as they entered the stableyard, and a small wiry man with leathery skin emerged from a doorway. His eyes crinkled in what Yani guessed was a rare sign of pleasure. "Amigo! So you are back. Have you found me many customers for this year?"

"Many will be coming later, but here`s an unexpected one from my journey. Yani, this is Senor Esteban, owner of the best stable of horses in the Pyrenees."

"What can I do for you, young sir?" Esteban asked, sizing up this serious looking youngster, gripping an unusual staff.

Yani explained he required a horse for about a month. His credit would cover the deposit, the hire and additional equipment such as a sleeping roll, saddlebags etc. "I'd better be prepared for the odd night out."

"You'll also need water bottles, basic rations, good maps, a compass...." and the suggestions continued, as Esteban warmed to his task.

"May I offer you lunch?" Salvador asked, "while Esteban is getting everything together for you. If you are going off into the hills, it may be sometime before you eat again."

A nearby bodega provided an appetizing choice of tapas and, within the hour, they were back at the stables loading everything into the saddlebags.

"That's wonderful," said Yani. "Now I'm equipped for anything."

"No trouble, it's been a great pleasure. If you need to contact me again, my daughter's house is the last one you pass as you leave on the Villanua road. I shall be staying with her for two weeks. Here's a small telescope. When you come back, return it and let me know how you got on. Take care, there are some rough people still in the hills and mountain valleys. The Ells didn't convert everyone!"

"That I know very well!" Yani said. "Thank you for everything! You've been most helpful."

Despite all the extra baggage, Sofia, his horse, tackled the hill north of Taca with a purposeful gait and Yani's hopes grew that soon he would be talking to Pedro Domingues, Estella's cave expert. It felt strange to be riding up into the mountains on his own, but at last he was doing something to find Mother.

The sun blazed down, the dry heat bouncing off the ground. Yani began to wish he had accepted the suggestion of a siesta before leaving, but his wish to find Pedro overpowered mere thoughts of personal comfort.

The road zigzagged endlessly upward. Roasting in the sun and with his head swimming, Yani plodded on till finally the waterfall, a white column falling from the heights, came into view.

Cresting a ridge, Yani made out a small group of grey houses near the cliff. A small lake, surrounded by green fields, lay below the waterfall to the right. Noticing that one building looked like an inn, he rode over to it, tethered Sofia near the door and went inside.

"Hola!" he shouted, and heard some footsteps coming from the back. A large sullen looking man appeared.

"I am looking for Pedro Domingues," Yani said politely, "Can you help me, senor?"

The man looked irritated and growled, "Pedro won`t be back for several days, perhaps a week or so. Why do you want him?"

"That`s my business," Yani replied, not caring for the man`s attitude. His heart sank at the news; a whole week to wait.

The innkeeper eyed him slyly, "I can rent you a room."

Yani nodded and agreed a modest sum for his stay and Sofia`s accommodation in the stables.

Still upset, he unsaddled and settled his mare in the stables, then took his saddlebags up to his room. It was simple but clean and boasted a shower in a corner. Refreshed after using it, Yani lay down and considered what he should do now.

The thought of sitting around doing nothing, when he was wound up for action, didn`t appeal. He could go back to Taca and ask Salvador if he knew of anyone with knowledge of where big cave complexes may be found. Tourists loved caves, but he doubted if his mother`s captor would have his caverns on the tourist trail. Yani needed someone with knowledge of unvisited caves, and such people were rare.

Downstairs, Santos, the surly innkeeper stood talking to his wife.

"I tell you, he`s the one!"

"What one?"

"The one mentioned in that letter to Pedro that I steamed open. He`s arrived early. Aranda wants him but won`t pay us a cent. On the other hand if Mila were to get him, and claim he captured him before he ever got here, Mila could negotiate with Aranda."

"You`re playing with fire, Santos, be very careful!"

Up in his room Yani got out his maps, spread them out, and circled in red all the marked grottoes and caves that were shown. Perhaps if he could find out which ones were not on the tourist list, that would make his search easier. His maps only dealt with this area of the vast mountain range: how many other areas might he have to search?

Sitting in Altania it had seemed a simple matter; go to the mountains, make enquires, and pinpoint suspected caves. Here the immensity of his task was overpowering. No wonder Zandor had said it would take time. It could take years!

He ate a solitary meal of slow cooked lamb, a local speciality, produced by the innkeeper`s wife, who was as talkative as her husband was silent. She was a small agile woman who scurried about the place, pouring beer for the few locals who came in. They all showed a sly interest in Yani but didn`t speak to him. Having said, "Good evening," to the first two who came in and received no response, Yani decided to remain silent.

"Just like Polonia," he thought.

When he got up to go to bed, the landlord suddenly appeared and gave him a large steaming mug. "A nightcap," he announced, "Sleep well!"

Taken aback by this unexpected generosity, Yani took it upstairs, where he sniffed suspiciously at it. There was an odd smell and, although the first sip tasted sweet, Yani decided he would be better without it and emptied it down the shower drain. He lay down without undressing and considered his options. An hour later he was dozing lightly, when he heard his door open quietly. He lay absolutely still, though quivering with the anticipation of being robbed, or attacked.

His right hand gripped his staff and he prepared to jump up and swing his arm round, striking whoever-it-was. However whoever-it-was stayed at the door and he heard whispering.

"Out like a dead man. I'll leave now and be back with Mila before dawn."

The door closed and Yani opened his eyes. His first impressions had been right; this man was not to be trusted.

What was to be done? He lay and heard a rider go off into the night and then someone else came upstairs and went along to the back of the inn, presumably the landlord's wife. Within half-an-hour he heard the faint sound of snoring. It was time to move!

He put everything in the saddlebags, including his rolled up rucksack then, slowly opening his door, crept downstairs. There was a nightlight burning on the desk and Yani paused to check that there was no one else around. Seeing some sheets of paper, he picked up a pen and scribbled, "Dear Landlord, I am leaving early and returning to Taca. Please ask Pedro to contact Esteban's stables when he returns. I have valuable work for him. I enclose some coins to cover my stay."

Outside there was only starlight, so it took a little time to recover his saddle from the stables. He was proficient enough with his staff to get it to glow a little, which helped. Sofia seemed pleased to see him. He threw on her saddle, tightened the girths, then led her quietly away from the group of houses.

Who else might be awake, he wondered. However, there was no call from any of the dark buildings, and it crossed Yani's mind that this village, like Polonia, might be used to mysterious night time travellers.

Reaching the roadway he turned right, away from Taca. There had been a small stand of trees further up the hill, which would be a good spot from which to watch the inn. Something useful might come out of learning more about those people who wished to capture him. They might even be the ones holding his mother.

Tethering Sofia behind the trees, Yani settled down to wait. One thing he had learnt during his time at Polonia, was patience. A deep silence lay over the hillside. The splash of the waterfall was too distant to carry up to him and he had nothing to watch except the wheeling stars. He tried to let his mind reach out to his mother, picturing her clearly in his mind but, since his visit to the Tower, he could not feel her presence anymore.

Hoofbeats roused him. The sky had paled, washing away the stars, and Yani could just discern a group of men riding up to the inn. They dismounted and went inside. Shortly after, angry shouts could be heard and the men came rushing out again, remounted and galloped off down the hill. Quietly Yani rose, mounted Sofia and set out to follow them.

Not far down the hill they turned to the left, along a smaller trail going eastwards. Yani held well back. He picked spots with a good view and used his pocket telescope.

The sun rose almost directly in front of him and it became much more difficult to see the riders. He stopped again behind some rocks and fumbled for his map. He spotted the trail he was on and traced where it was going. A few kilometres ahead it split into three. He needed to know which one they took, for beyond that there were no more divisions. That should pinpoint their destination, then he could return to Taca and wait to see if Pedro got in touch. At least he would have learned something about some of his enemies. Every little thing could help.

The gap had widened considerably, and Yani felt safe in going forward. As the sun rose it became easier to see, and far ahead Yani spied the men entering the shadow of some trees. The map had shown woods this side of the junction. If he moved quietly to the far side of the trees, he could remain in hiding and spot which way they chose.

Yani rode into the wood. It was quite dense and branches formed an arch over the track. He picked his way carefully, in case the riders had stopped for any reason. Suddenly a body fell from above, grabbed him and threw him to the ground. Two other figures jumped out of the bushes, one snatched the startled Sofia`s reins, and the other helped his companion subdue a vigorous Yani. They wrapped a rope around him before tying his hands in front of him.

A broadset, rough looking man seized Yani by the chin.

"You've been following us. Why? What's your name?"

"Let go of me! Is this how you treat visitors to your mountains?"

"I asked your name, nuisance!"

"Alfonso Delguardo. My father is an important—"

"Your name is Yan t'Ell, I recognize Santos's description. You've caused me much trouble so your price has just gone up! Let's get you under lock and key. Blindfold him then seat him on his horse but ride in front holding that rope."

"Mila, shouldn't we make him walk?"

Mila, obviously the leader, sneered at the speaker. "Franci, you've less brains than your horse. Do you want to spend all day walking? We've been up since two and should get back as fast as we can. Do as I say and stop trying to think!"

Suitably subdued, Franci put Yani back on Sofia. Holding onto the rope tied round Yani's waist, Franci then mounted his own horse and the cavalcade set off at a brisk pace.

Behind his blindfold Yani raged at himself. How could he have been so stupid? These men, experienced bandits, would have been aware of anyone trying to track them. He only hoped that they wanted to trade him, and that might lead him closer to his mother. He tried to shut out the awful despair he felt at being a captive again and almost welcomed the ropes chafing his wrists; he deserved all the discomfort he got.

After what seemed an eternity, their pace slowed and Yani heard other voices greeting them. They had arrived—but where? Lifted down but still blindfolded, he was led to a room and dumped on a bed. Mila proceeded to handcuff Yani's right hand to the iron bedstead before loosening the rope from his wrists.

"That will keep you in place!" he grunted. "You'll get food and water if you keep quiet, but none if you make trouble."

The door opened and Franci came in carrying Yani's saddlebags, his staff hanging in its harness.

"Yes," grinned Mila, "better leave them here—too many thieves around outside!" and he laughed as he took Franci out.

Yani loosened his blindfold, then lay back and tried to fight the self-contempt that washed over him. How could he have been so careless, he didn`t dare imagine what Zandor would have to say to him.

CHAPTER TEN

1

Squalls

Far to the south, Turias and his friends had also run into trouble. The first morning's sail had gone well, with a light westerly wind behind them. By midday this had died however, and the sky to the south had acquired an ominous coppery colour.

"I don't much like the look of that," Turias remarked. "Something nasty might blow up during the night. I'll take the first watch, then Pasco then Ragore. There's little wind now but that could change quickly.

"Aye aye skipper!" said Pasco, getting into the nautical mood.

The first two watches passed quietly but, with Ragore on deck, things changed dramatically. Out of nowhere, a swirling gust of wind struck the little yacht laying her over alarmingly. Ragore threw up his arm to protect his head as the boom swung over but ducked too late. He shouted as he fell sideways. Turias leapt up from below. He grabbed the tiller, steadied the yacht and called to Pasco to come and attend to Ragore.

"I'm afraid his arm's broken," Pasco said a few minutes later. "I've immobilized it for the time being, but it requires proper treatment."

"In that case," Turias replied, "we'd better return—if this storm allows us."

The sea had risen with the wind, hungry waves leapt round chucking cascades of spray over them and they were hard put to keep their small craft under control. Then, as suddenly as it had struck them, the squall departed. Light appeared in the eastern sky and the choppy seas took on shape and a little colour.

Ragore had been laid down below on a bunk and strapped in. Turias went down to check and returned to say he was sleeping.

"I gave him a powerful pain killer," Pasco said, "Sleep's the best thing for him just now. You look pretty tired yourself, like the giant after the beanstalk was chopped down!"

"Don`t look in a mirror just now," Turias advised him, "You`d get a terrible fright! Fortunately the wind`s swung round so, if it holds, we could be back in Altania by nightfall. Let`s get some sail on her, then you get some rest. You can relieve me in four hours."

Their arrival back at Altania was in sad contrast to their exuberant departure. Ragore was miserable at having spoilt their long planned trip and blamed himself.

"I tried to save my head. Perhaps I shouldn`t have bothered," he added miserably.

"Well, it's not much of a head, or face come to that," Pasco remarked, "but we`ve all grown used to it, so you probably did the right thing!"

"I`ll deal with him later for you," Turias assured Ragore. "He knows you can`t hit back at the moment. These little chaps are always the cheekiest."

Having settled Ragore in the accident ward, Turias and Pasco went off to tell Yani what had happened. Unable to find him, they went to see Arlinda. Hearing their story and, though sorry to learn of Ragore`s accident, she was much more alarmed by Yani`s disappearance.

"Something`s been brewing up in him for some time," she stated. "He`s always been obsessed about his mother`s plight and, since he came back from the Tower, he imagines he`s become a fully grown adult overnight."

Turias shrugged. "I thought he might have gone off with that girl he likes, Estella her name is, but she`s still here studying. I checked, and she`s hard at work."

"Let me make some enquiries. You lads need some rest after your exertions so give me an hour or so to contact people while you relax. These are good chairs for dozing in if you

101

recline them. I'll see Ragore later and tell him what's happening. It'll take his mind off his own problems."

Arlinda went through to her office and contacted the tube station. Yes, they told her, a young Ell had taken the tube to Taca yesterday.

Next, she opened her V-phone and contacted Zandor. She explained the situation and added that Turias and Pasco were now at a loose end and wanted to help.

"I'd have thought he had more sense," Zandor said. "Stupid boy—"

"He thinks he's all grown up now, after the Tower."

"Hmmmph!"

"Turias and Pasco want to come up and help search for him."

"I'm not sure—"

"At least they could escort him home once you've found him."

"Well at the moment I'm deep in the mountains, and there are no tubes between here and Taca. It will take me all today and half the night to ride there, but I could meet the lads in Taca tomorrow morning. There's a hostelry at the station. I'll join them there."

2

Prisoner

In the sultry night, thunder prowled among the hills, grumbling like a hungry tiger. Heavy spots of rain splattered the courtyard. Yani lay on the hard, dirty mattress wondering how to escape. He had been fed and, under supervision, had been allowed to use the common washroom. He thought he was in an old farm, since he'd heard goats bleating. He wanted to examine the bedstead as he thought part of it might come loose. One half of the handcuff was attached to the iron bedstead. If he could separate the upright he could slide the cuff off. He struggled with this for some time in the dark until

102

a strange noise stopped him. A small light appeared in the fireplace, followed by a pair of spindly legs and then, finally, a dirty imp, white teeth shining in a blackened face.

It put its finger to its lips and made an unnecessary "Shhhhh!" sound.

Yani gazed in wonder at this sooty apparition creeping towards him. It put its mouth close to Yani's ear and said, "I'm little Peter!" as if that explained everything.

Yani raised his eyebrows in a silent question.

"This was my home till these men came. They killed my uncle and aunty, but they didn't kill me as I'm useful with the goats. They think I'm stupid." The urchin produced a fearsome smile, "but I'm not. I'm nine now, and very clever! If I get you out, will you take me with you?" Fascinated by this unlikely helper, Yani nodded.

The whispers continued, "Mila's gone off to fix your ransom, so we have time. I've heard them talking; they think you're worth a lot of money." He shone the light on Yani and little Peter's brow frowned. "You don't look worth much to me!"

"Never mind the compliments," Yani whispered, "how will I get out?

"Leave it to me," said the sooty imp, "I suppose you'll need your horse?"

Yani nodded. "She's strong enough to carry us both."

"Be ready at this time tomorrow. Goodnight!" and Peter departed the way he had come, scuffing the floor to disguise any footprints he might have left. The floor was so dirty anyway that any trace of his visit was unlikely to be noticed.

Yani wondered if he had been dreaming and pinched himself quite firmly. Eventually he fell asleep and had wild dreams in which hordes of tiny imps attacked Mila and his men, swarming all over them with tiny swords. Then they turned on him and started pricking him, just as fiercely. Yani woke to find he was being bitten by a number of ants that had invaded his bed. Restricted as he was, he scrambled about vigorously and eventually managed to kill them. Still more

103

arrived and at last the door was unlocked by the surly Franci, carrying a lamp.

"What's all the noise about?" he grumbled then, seeing the ants, went out and returned with a spray that soon dispersed them. "We don't want you marked, do we? Valuable goods, Mila says!" and he spat. "Me? I would give you a good thrashing anyway, but Mila would notice," and he went out and locked the door.

Dawn arrived soon and Yani spent a long day wondering if his midget rescuer would appear that night. At last he was given an evening meal and locked up as before. He waited and waited, every moment seeming like an hour.

At last he heard the door open and his heart sank. Franci had come back to check on him. Peter would be caught and...

"Shhhh!" came a familiar whisper, and Peter's outline appeared against the faint light from the door.

"Where's that handcuff? I've brought the key!"

"Here," said Yani, his heart beating with relief. "What about Franci?"

"Oh I gave him something to make him sleep!" announced the child. He giggled, "He won't half have a sore head tomorrow! If he wakes at all," he added sinisterly. "Follow me, but bring your bags."

Yani followed his rescuer out of the room and along a corridor. A door at the end led into a pitch dark yard, but Peter took hold of Yani's hand and led him unerringly to the stables where a small light burned. Here Sofia stood, already saddled, and Yani threw on the saddlebags, his staff still attached through its loop.

"Wait here for a moment," Peter said, "There's one thing I must do before we leave, then I'll come back and lead you out of here."

Yani waited impatiently, staff in hand, till the boy reappeared.

"Now," said Peter, still in a whisper, "you can rescue me!" and quietly they walked out of the farmyard. Five minutes later, Yani climbed up into the saddle and, bending down, pulled Peter up behind him.

"Which way to Taca?" he asked.

"Straight on for an hour or so, then we come to a crossroads. The left track goes south to Taca."

"Why are you helping me?" Yani asked, turning to look at Peter.

"Last year these men came to our farm and killed my uncle and aunty. They were all the family I've had since Mum and Dad were killed," and for a moment the mouth turned down. "I hate them! They are bad people so, tonight when I made their drink, I put something in it." Peter gave a happy smile, "I think it was poisonous!"

"What?" exclaimed Yani, "You think you've killed them?"

"I hope so. They all sleep in an outhouse and I locked the door after building up the fire. While you were waiting in the stable, I put something over the chimney top so perhaps they'll suffocate—if the poison doesn't work," he added cheerfully.

Yani could think of absolutely nothing to say to this dangerous, resourceful character. They rode on through the night, companioned only by wind and stars.

3

Taca

Turias and Pasco had arrived at Taca to find a stern looking Zandor waiting for them. "Did you know of this tomfoolery?"

"Indeed not," Turias replied, adding "or we would not have let him go alone!"

Zandor snorted. "Lads that think they've become men overnight! There must be more Earth blood in you all than I thought. Anyway, you've offered to help. What's your first suggestion?"

Pasco cleared his throat. "Well sir," he said, "I thought, that is we thought, that Yani would need a horse, so perhaps if we find out the various stables…"

"Excellent! I have just done so and learned that, two days ago, Yani hired a horse from Esteban's stables. He was introduced by a fellow called Salvador, who is staying nearby at his daughter's house. I think we should visit him first, after we've got you extra legs. Esteban's lined up a couple of good beasts for you. Follow me!"

They collected their horses, another two mares that Kuzak eyed with approval, and made their way to where Salvador was staying. He met them at the door.

"Esteban called to tell me you were coming over. May I introduce my daughter Janine, I've explained the situation to her."

Janine, a slim lady with auburn hair, greeted them warmly. "Please come in. May I offer you some refreshment while we talk? I've made coffee but—."

"Coffee would be excellent, thank you, but we are anxious to find where my grandson has gone."

Salvador nodded. He laid out a large-scale map on the table and circled Taca with a marker pen.

"You must understand that I only had the pleasure of a brief chat with your grandson and he didn't say where he was going. However he left on the road to Pilgrims' Gap. If he was aiming to go there, he left too late to reach it in a day. We had a little lunch before he left."

Zandor decided this was a man he could trust, so he explained briefly that Yani was attempting to find his mother. Salvador's eyes widened, "An Ell lady, held in captivity, I've never heard of such a thing!"

"That's what's so worrying. Someone must have acquired some Ell technology, in order to hold her. The other worry is they must be planning to use it when we are gone."

"But we are being trained to stay and see that doesn't happen," Turias said in his deepest voice.

"Who are "we"?" Salvador enquired, eyeing this young giant with interest.

"The last generation of half-ells. All with Ell mothers," said Pasco, speaking for the first time.

Salvador frowned, "It`s true there are still a number of towns and villages that stayed aloof from Ell influence, but generally they know better than to make trouble. Yani looked pretty competent to me."

Zandor shook his head. "My worry is that if Yani is caught by whoever holds his mother, there will be no need to keep Elaire alive. It's a young Ell male they`ll want."

A horrified silence fell. Turias looked at Pasco; they hadn`t thought of that.

"Indeed," Zandor added, "anyone of you would do. If you were captured, and the right mind-bending drugs used, our enemies would have what they want, a soldier with an Ell mother and full Ell talents. None of you should venture alone into marginal lands until you are fully trained."

"Whatever you plan to do, please make my house your base," said Janine. "Father`s island, Marmorian, is too far down river—"

"Where you would be equally welcome," Salvador interjected

"But that is putting you to too much trouble," Zandor objected, but was totally overruled.

"Don`t waste time arguing with my daughter," Salvador laughed, "She has a will of iron!"

Zandor smiled and gave in gracefully.

Janine looked at Turias, "I just hope the bed is big enough."

"Oh, he can always stick his feet out the window. It won`t be the first time." Pasco put in. "Besides, the air stays fresher!"

"Let me make a call," Salvador said. "Juan, the innkeeper at Pilgrims` Gap, will know if Yani arrived in the village. He`s well informed."

Juan`s face appeared on the V-phone and Salvador asked him if a young student had reached the village.

"Not as far as I know, but let me make enquiries. I`ll call you back shortly."

"If you find him he`s to call me back urgently," Salvador said.

"You must eat while you wait," Janine insisted.

Later, after they had consumed much of an excellent ham, Juan called back to say that no youngster had arrived in the village from the south. They then discussed where the search should be concentrated.

"There is a trail going eastwards from just below the waterfall and it joins with another that runs north-east from here," Salvador pointed to the map. "Not that there is much up there, only a few old farms and an ancient monastery."

At that moment the V-phone rang, and Salvador answered it. Esteban's walnut face appeared.

"The young lad's here," he said. "Just arrived and he's got a small creature with him."

Zandor jumped up. "Don't let him out of your sight!" he begged. "I shall come across and fetch him." Janine laid her hand on his shoulder.

"Just before you go rushing off, remember he was only trying to help you. What he needs is mothering, not lecturing. You bring him back to me!"

Zandor grunted something inaudible, then gave a huge sigh of relief.

"Yes, you're quite right, but he's caused everyone so much worry and trouble.."

"Never mind. Bring him here and the creature he's found. What can it be, a wild cat perhaps?"

Half-an-hour later a very subdued Yani was presented to the assembled company, together with a small, remarkably dirty urchin, who looked at them all from a pair of bright eyes. He inspected Turias in amazement.

"Wow!" he said, "You're even bigger than Yani said. Don't you keep banging your head on things?"

"This," said Zandor in a loud voice, "is little Peter, and if you can get him to stop talking for a moment I shall be very grateful."

Janine said, "Welcome, both of you! Let's get some of that dirt off, then I expect you'll be hungry."

"Not half," said Peter, staring at the remains of the ham.

"Peter, Yani, come with me," and Janine led them away.

As soon as they had gone the questions started. Zandor raised his hand.

"I've only heard a little of it, but it seemed that Yani was seized by some brigands and rescued by Peter, who may have killed them all."

There was a stunned silence.

"Killed them all? Peter killed the brigands? How?" Salvador spoke faintly.

"Probably talked them to death. But the child keeps saying that Yani saved him. I don't understand it."

"No doubt all will be revealed, after they've eaten."

The return of a cleaner Yani and a scrubbed Peter, still in his dirty clothes, stopped the speculation. Peter's subsequent attack on the ham was breathtaking.

"Yes, well, we can start with table manners tomorrow," Janine remarked. "He's no parents, and the uncle and aunt who took him in were killed by the brigands. They kept him to skivvy for them. Anyway," she announced calmly, "he's going to stay with us now. He likes it here."

She lifted her eyebrows and looked at her father. "That's all right with you?"

Wide-eyed Salvador nodded. "But you do remember what he did to his late hosts?"

"Yes, he told me. He 'did them in.'"

The remains of the ham having vanished, Peter found another use for his tongue. "Well," he said defiantly, "they killed my aunty, nice woman she was." He sniffed a little. "And my uncle," he added, as an afterthought. "Then Yani came, he saved me!"

Attention switched to Yani, who had barely said a word. "I'll explain in a little while," he mumbled.

Janine spoke firmly. "Yes, well, I think it's time Peter got some sleep. Peter you come with me and I'll find you a bed."

Peter stared up at her, "A real bed?"

Zandor went over and lifted Peter up until their faces were level.

"I'm not sure who rescued whom," he said, "but I do know that, but for you, I would have lost my grandson." His voice broke a little, "and that would have been too much to bear. Thank you, little Peter," and he kissed the astonished child on his forehead. Wide eyed, and for once silenced, Peter was led away.

"Now Yani, for goodness sake explain." Pasco demanded, "Whatever has gone on?"

Yani looked round at the expectant faces, cleared his throat, swallowed and said, "First of all, I am so sorry for the worry I've caused. I only wanted to help but I hadn't realized that I might be putting my mother's life in danger, if her captor got hold of me." He stopped as tears came to his eyes, then shook his head and recounted his adventures.

When he had finished, Pasco shook his head. "I must say you have a very active guardian angel!"

"With unusual instruments," added Turias dryly

"Peter's heart's in the right place," Salvador said, "though I might have a problem explaining a farm with poisoned bodies to the authorities up here."

Zandor nodded, "They may have difficulty seeing it as we do. I suggest that we all ride out to this place tomorrow, leaving Peter with Janine, if we may…"

"Absolutely," she said. "I want to get him properly cleaned then kitted out in decent clothes."

"We must tell him not to speak of this to anyone just now. If you will come with me under my protection," here Zandor lifted his staff, "we can deal with any brigands left. We may even find some useful evidence at the farm to aid our search for Elaire. If nothing else we can remove Peter's cover from the chimney, then any later official investigation will assume they all died from food poisoning."

"I will not alert the authorities for some weeks," said Salvador. "I will simply say that Peter was found by a young student and brought to me for shelter. Finding out where he came from was not easy. In time, when he has grown up, he can claim the farm as his uncle's only heir."

110

"Justice will then be done," Zandor said.

Early next morning, a small cavalcade of riders left Taca, heading north. It was another glorious day, cool at first but warming up as they progressed. Much of the time their way was sheltered by trees, but when they crossed a series of ridges, the ground became bare and rocky, reflecting the heat in waves. By the time they reached the junction with the track from the west, it was noon. Despite the heat they pressed on, ever watchful, but seeing no other sign of human life. Lower ground brought them through a small forest of birches beyond which signs of old cultivation appeared.

At sometime in the past this land had been farmed, and it was not long before they saw a group of buildings straight ahead. Slowly, alert for any attack, they rode into the central yard. "Hallo!" Turias bellowed.

Some faint echoes came back, but otherwise there was no sign of life. Yani pointed to a building adjacent to the stables, "That's where the men lived. Look, there is something over the chimney!"

Zandor rode up to the building and dismounted. "There's a key in the lock," he said, and tried to unlock it. "It's not locked," he said, surprised.

The door swung open and a horrible smell hit them. Zandor covered his face with a cloth and went in. Quite soon he came out again and closed the door. He removed the key. "No one alive in there." He looked round, "Where's Pasco?"

"Up here," came a voice from the roof. "Watch out!" and a piece of board came hurtling down. Salvador went across and carried it over to a pile of old timber.

"That's disposed of the evidence," Zandor remarked, "now let us see if there is any sign of a connection with other groups."

The rest of the day spent investigating the farm thoroughly. Little of interest was found apart from a map of Andorra. It seemed that the old monastery had been a virtual ruin for years and showed no signs of habitation. The main hall was in better condition and Salvador suggested they spend the night there, but keeping the horses in the stables. "We will need to set a watch," he said, "in case this fellow Mila returns."

"It would be most helpful if he did," Zandor said.

Pasco, looking apologetic, slapped his hand to his brow. "I didn`t mention that I found some fresh horse turds at the east gate. I thought they might have been one of ours, but they looked a little older!"

"Pasco is an expert in such matters," Turias said proudly.

"If this fellow returned before us and found all his men dead....that`s why the door was not locked! He`s taken fright and ridden off. We won`t see him again. He must have arrived early this morning. Perhaps we can find some tracks when it gets light." Outside the light was failing and the evening air brought a refreshing coolness.

In case their surmise was wrong, a watch was set, but the night passed uneventfully. The silence of the mountains was almost palpable, broken only now and then by the squeal of some animal caught by a predator. In the dawn`s light Salvador, Pasco and Zandor examined the ground at the east gate.

"Look," Salvador spoke softly, "you can see that someone tethered his horse here. Close by there was a water trough, fed by a pipe from a spring. It overflowed and the ground was slightly muddy.

"There are boot marks," Pasco pointed out, "going towards the farm. I`m afraid I didn`t see them yesterday, I`m very sorry."

"It would not have made any difference," Zandor said. "He must have left hours before we arrived and be far away by now. There`s nothing more for us here, and we have taken up too much of your time," he added, turning to Salvador.

"It has been my pleasure," Salvador said. "I only wish we had found more evidence. Before we leave we should turn the goats loose to fend for themselves."

"That would be sensible," Zandor said. "Now Andorra might be a lead, but it`s further east than where I intended to search. Anyway let`s return to see how Janine has managed with Peter. I trust he hasn`t harmed any of your good townfolk." During the ride back, Zandor issued precise instructions to the students.

"It`s my job to search for Elaire, and it`s your task to acquire all the skills you can. Soon we must leave this beautiful planet, then you and your fellows will be the only line of defence against anyone misusing Ell technology. You must prepare yourselves properly!

"By this autumn you will be ready and, if I still haven`t found Elaire, your first duty will be to come and help me. Turias, you are needed in America, Arlinda has plans for Lucy, so that would leave Ragore and Pasco to join Yani if they are willing."

"And now?" Turias asked.

"And now you will all return to Altania and finish your course. I will pursue this fellow Domingues and quiz him on caves. I will also go to Andorra, but you three must leave this evening for Altania! I want you all well out of harm`s way."

They arrived back at Janine`s house to say their farewells to Janine and Peter, who was most upset to learn that Yani was leaving him.

"But you will come down to Altania and visit me. Salvador comes once a year so, next time, he could bring you and Janine, to see what it is like down there," Yani said. Somewhat mollified by this, Peter then launched into a tale of his morning in Taca with Janine. Esteban had promised him riding lessons but there were certain shops where Janine had agreed not to return with Peter until he had better control of his tongue.

CHAPTER ELEVEN

1

Hector

Outside the mountain, sheets of rain lashed the greystone cliffs, sending waterfalls cascading into the misty depths. Inside an entirely different scene unfolded. A frightened man stood in a deep amphitheatre, clutching his sole weapon, a long forked triton. Spotlights shone down, leaving the watchers above in shadow. An ominous rumbling came from a side tunnel—something dangerous approached. A sharp acid smell stung his nose. Eyes glittering and arms tensed, the man shivered; beads of fear stood out on his brow.

A vast shape shambled out into the light and the man gasped. Hairy like a grizzly bear, it had long gorilla-like arms with hands whose fingers ended in fearsome looking claws. The mouth stretched wide, showing fangs dripping long slimy strings of saliva. It stood upright and peered about suspiciously. Spying the man, its eyes narrowed and a low growling noise raised the hair on the necks of the watchers. The man`s legs trembled and he looked up desperately into the darkness. "For pity`s sake, Krask, get me out of here," he screamed. "I`ll do anything!"
"You`ve already done too much, Draach. You alerted the Ells to danger. You acted too soon and against my wishes. You will now serve as an example to any who might think of crossing me! They too will meet Hector. Don`t you think he`s a fine fellow?"

Distracted by the voices the creature had stopped, then, uttering hoarse grunts, advanced upon its victim. Draach jabbed at it with his weapon and it jumped back quickly. It began to circle the man slowly, feinting with its long arms but keeping its body back from the sharp prongs.

After some time Draach`s legs began to tire. "I have to kill it soon or I`m dead, "he thought. "It`s now or never!" and he

114

leapt forward, lunging straight at the creature's chest. Hector was faster. A great arm swung down, batting the triton aside and leaving the man defenceless. The other arm swept in and the claws fastened around Draach's throat, cutting off his agonized screams. Hector lifted his victim up and then the terrible jaws started to tear the man to pieces. Krask turned to Horrold, the genetic scientist responsible for the breeding programme. "What about the Ells' vibration defence?"

"The gorrat has no conscience to be stimulated, so there can be no effect."

"Splendid, Horrold, splendid! Accelerate the breeding programme! We'll keep that fool Mila for another lesson."

2

Martial Arts

During August, Yani spent most of his time training in various forms of combat. While fighting scarcely existed anymore, sporting competitions in the martial arts were popular. Yani was determined that, next time he went north, he would be as well trained as possible. No second-rate bunch of villains would capture him again! He reported to Estella that Pablo had been missing and that he had been sent back to finish his courses.

"But I'm going back again at the end of next month," he promised her, "and as you are going home then, I'll not be far away. Once I've found Mother—"

"But you can base your search from Father's place."

"That's far too kind, surely—"

"He will insist!" Estella said emphatically.

The month wore on and Yani drove himself ever harder. "Really, Yani," Ragore complained one day, "with all these vigorous activities you involve yourself in, we don't see much of you."

"A little physical activity would do you a lot of good," Turias commented.

Ragore looked alarmed, "Now you are not going to drag me off to play some of these dreadful games you and that squirt Pasco get involved in. Last April I thought I would be torn to pieces. It took weeks before I stopped having nightmares."

Pasco giggled. "You should have seen him, Yani. A friendly game of rugby football and, when he was thrown the ball and saw the opposition coming for him, he panicked."

"I took commonsense, evasive action," Ragore protested with all the dignity he could muster.

"But you ran the wrong way! You were meant to run through them, forwards, not backwards!"

Ragore covered his face with his hands and shuddered.

"I can still see that gigantic pack coming for me. I think I behaved with great intelligence. Lucy thought so—and she's the wise one here."

"At least it makes it certain you won't be picked again! I assume that was your intention anyway."

"Never crossed my mind," Ragore said, wide-eyed and innocent. .

The five students had discussions on every subject they could think of, often after an evening beach barbecue. Sitting round the remains of their fire with the waves pounding and the fathomless canopy of stars wheeling far above, they would talk the night away. Yani told stories of his escape and the horrors of his life in Polonia.

"But in the old days many youngsters were treated like that," said Ragore, "and even those lucky enough to be students like us had their problems. We have few money problems..."

"I beg your pardon," Turias interjected, "was it your double then, who had to borrow from me last week, and not for the first time!"

"And before that it was from me," said Lucy. "He said it was for a present for a special girl." They both looked accusingly at Ragore, who shrugged. "Well, you others seem to manage better than me. My researches into the best value

116

places doesn't come cheap, you know, and to whom do you come for advice...?"

"At heart you are just a martyr slaving away for others. Have you ever thought of becoming a monk and...."

Ragore chocked.

Yani, laughing, said that he had already made arrangements for Ragore to be taken to a retreat where they lived on bread and water. "I've paid for a month's stay for you," he announced. "Don't thank me, it's a birthday present. They will come and get you first thing tomorrow. Perhaps we should put on the manacles now. Turias will you help me?"

"No need, he's fainted!"

Later Yani raised the matter closest to his heart.

"Remember Zandor has agreed I can join him at the beginning of October."

"I hope you don't intend to leave us behind again," Pasco snapped.

"Well, I know Turias has to go to America, and I'm not sure Ragore would enjoy living rough, but you'd be very welcome."

"When did I ever put my comfort before helping you lot?" Ragore demanded. "Who broke his arm steering the boat while his friends slept? Who....?" before he was shouted down .

Yani raised his voice. "Right, that's settled! Ragore's arm has mended so we three can travel north together and meet Grandpa at Pilgrims' Gap, near to Estella's home, on the first of October. Estella has offered us support from her father's place: she suggested that could be a useful base for us."

"Very decent," said Pasco, "You must be very persuasive, Yani!" He looked at his sister, "Would you like to come?"

Lucy frowned, "I'm not sure, this sounds like boy's stuff. I'll probably stay here and do some sailing."

3

Staff Skills

Arlinda gave them their first staff instruction in Altania's concert hall.

"Magic?" they asked Arlinda, "You are going to teach us magic?"

"Well, that's what humans would call it, but its all part of being an Ell. You know that our brains generate powerful thought waves—you have probably noticed how obedient animals are to you. While these can be strengthened by pointing with your fingers, they are multiplied a hundred fold by using a proper Ell staff. Any long object helps, but these are special."

Arlinda now produced five staves of varying lengths and gave one to each of them. While all had the appearance of polished wood, there were subtle differences in markings and colour.

"Hold the head firmly against your forehead, close your eyes, and stand still for three minutes. Breathe slowly and deeply, open your minds and relax."

They did so and a gentle tingling started inside their heads, followed by a motion, as if they were flying. Very far off, they heard the shimmering of crystal bells, then a faint but haunting music, and a deep sense of peace flowed into their hearts.

"Now you are attuned to your staff," Arlinda said, "and it to you."

"That music!" exclaimed Lucy, "it was so beautiful I could listen to it for ever."

"I could hardly hear it," said Turias, Ragore and Pasco agreeing with him.

Arlinda looked at Lucy, "Can you remember any of the melody?" she asked.

Frowning in concentration Lucy began to hum softly. Hesitatingly the others joined her, each singing a different tune, yet all blended into an enchanting melody.

"Now raise your staffs together," Arlinda commanded, "and think of the music."

Gently at first, the music returned, intermingled with the chiming of bells, slowly rising up to fill the hall as if a huge orchestra was playing. Swelling to a magnificent crescendo it again dwindled away down to a chord of exquisite, haunting beauty.

"Such is the true language of the Ells," said Arlinda, "but your staff also has practical uses. If you are attacked by anyone wanting to harm you, you can direct a flash of energy at them. However that takes a lot out of you mentally. It is less tiring to create calming vibrations, which you saw Zandor use once. However that works best with humans, as it relies on arousing the conscience in people. That bubble you saw Zandor throw over these men stimulated a reaction from them. The harm they had done to others rose up and overpowered them with remorse."

She smiled at the expectant faces before her.

"Now you are equipped to defend yourselves and go out into the world. I will remain here and organize Turias's American visit. Yani, you, Ragore and Pasco should gather everything for your journey north. If there is any further news from Zandor I shall call you on the V-phone. He did mention he might visit Salvador at Marmorian, his island. I have spoken to Salvador but he's heard nothing so far.

Arlinda embraced each of them in turn. Yani had only been back for a few months and now he was leaving again. She turned away quickly to hide the tears in her eyes. "Silly old fool," she said to herself, "they will do well and Zandor is there.

CHAPTER TWELVE

1

Into the Mountains

On the twenty-eighth of September, Yani, Ragore and Pasco travelled by tube to Taca, where they hired horses from Esteban's stables.

"I'm not sure how long we shall be needing them," Yani said.

Esteban shrugged, "That's not a problem, you've left a good deposit and we'll deal with the rest when you return. I wish you good travelling."

"Good travelling indeed," growled Ragore that afternoon, as they plodded their way up into the mountains through howling wind and battering rain.

"This is good for the soul, especially yours," grinned Pasco, "It could do with some hardship and cleansing!"

Ragore told Pasco what to do with his opinions.

"But I belong to the North," Pasco explained, "these storms invigorate me – think how good you'll feel this evening, having beaten the wind and rain, to arrive at a stout inn with roaring fires and splendid food."

"I'm busy enough thinking how to stop rain trickling down my neck," grumbled Ragore. "Can you even see where the way is?"

The wind shrieked as the storm increased in fury till the driving rain obscured the track. A cliff face looming up on their right offered some protection, but the path veered left.

"Look," shouted Yani, who lead the way, "there's a sheltered spot there against the cliff." He turned off the track and, dismounting, led them into a dry area created by a hollow in the cliff face. A narrow opening lay at the back and Yani went in. To his delight it opened into a cave, dark, gloomy, but dry.

Thankful to be out of the storm, the other two followed. The cave stretched back for some fifteen metres, resembling a huge half barrel lying on its side.

"At least we're prepared for unexpected stops—that's my mountain training!" Pasco announced smugly. Ragore, looking like a survivor from a shipwreck, sneezed violently.

Their emergency kit included bedrolls for themselves, oats for the horses now sheltering under the overhang, packs of rations, lamps and an odd looking bird cage which Yani was assembling. He set it carefully in the middle of the floor, packed it with stones, then touched it with his staff. Very soon it hummed and began to glow brighter and brighter. The stones became incandescent with heat and soon the whole cavern was warming up. Wet cloaks were spread out to dry and everyone became more cheerful.

"Getting back to nature is all very well," Ragore said, between more sneezes, "but a bit of modern technology helps ease the pain."

They heated water and soon were enjoying hot mugs of onion soup. Pasco went out several times to check the weather but told them there was little chance of it clearing before morning. Yani said, "We can always check the forecast with Arlinda but I would rather like to complete our journey without outside help." Pasco agreed, but Ragore said he was all for any outside help they could get.

"You've led too sheltered a life, my friend," Yani stated, "a short stay at my old village would have toughened you up!"

"Any more suggestions like that and you can sleep outside."

Resigned to staying where they were till morning, they studied maps of the Pyrenees, showing details of Zandor's travels. "Nothing positive yet" he had reported, but he was suspicious about an area lying to the north of Pilgrims' Gap.

"Look," said Yani pointing, "that's near Estella's home!"

"That'll give you something to look forward to," grinned Pasco.

Yani flushed slightly, then suggested that they got some sleep while waiting for the storm to blow itself out. They spread out their bedrolls and settled down. It seemed strange to be lying around a glowing brazier listening to the howling wind outside but, tired by their ride through the storm, they were soon asleep.

Late in the night, Yani woke to see a tall figure beckoning to him. Though astonished, Yani sensed it was friendly. Quietly he rose and followed it to the back of the cave. There, lying on a ledge was a long object wrapped in linen. Yani picked it up, unwrapped it and found a staff similar to his own.

"Lay your own staff beside it," murmured the figure, "this is the rainbow staff, seven in one, promised to you by the Elders. The controlling jewel you already have." Yani laid his staff down and saw the two merge into one.

The voice continued, "Here is your personal Bee. You control it with your mind. To see what it can see—just close your eyes." and he pressed his thumb hard against Yani's forehead. It pricked him for a second. "That is the implant, now I wish you farewell." The figure then turned and walked out into the storm. Totally bemused, Yani gazed after him then, carrying the staff, returned to his bedroll.

Waking in the morning, he wondered if it had only been a dream. He picked the staff up and went to the entrance where the light was brighter. The storm had departed, leaving a pale blue washed sky and fresher air. He examined the staff and saw that, while the difference may not be noticed by his companions, it was heavier and darker than his previous one.

"How do I learn to use you?" he wondered. He pressed its head against his own and, as with his previous staff, he felt a floating sensation, but then he heard, not music, but a voice inside his head.

"Now we have contact," it said. "I am the gift the Elders promised you. Being of incredibly dense material I need an anti-gravity device to counteract my weight. Indeed I could easily lift you. Time will teach you to trust my artificial intelligence."

At the same time, memories of distant ages came to Yani. He felt himself to be the latest in a long line of wise men who had used this staff in ancient times.

"But I am not a wise man," Yani thought, and immediately felt the answer, "Not yet."

He went inside, still puzzled, and heated some water to make hot drinks.

"Wake up you two. The weather's fine, just some mist about. We can pack up and go."

"Slavedriver," Ragore grumbled.

2

Lucy alone

In Altania, with her friends away, Lucy went round to see Estella. She found her still hard at work, but with several piles of paper bound up with string.

"Estella, haven't you heard of holidays?"

Estella seemed rather flustered by Lucy's arrival. "Oh, I was just sorting out some things to take home to study."

Lucy shook her head. "You put us all to shame. Anyway I was thinking over your suggestion that I come north with you. I know I said no, but it would surprise the lads when they get there—and I miss them already. When will you travel?"

"I hope to leave in three days," said Estella and, leaning forward, she grasped Lucy's hands in hers and shook them warmly. "I'm so pleased you've changed your mind."

"Well I feel we are becoming better friends, but there is still a bit of mystery about you too."

Estella looked down, then she withdrew her hands and stood up. "Yes, I suppose I am a bit of an enigma to you all. It's just I've had so much to learn and my father doesn't countenance failure."

Lucy was surprised. "In this day and age! Isn't that a relic from the bad old days?"

"Ah well, perhaps we are still a little old fashioned in the Pyrenees!"

Lucy shrugged, "All families have their own ways," she said. "Now I'd better go and get organized."

Later she tried to contact Arlinda, only to find that she had gone to see Turias in America and would not be back for a week. Lucy left a message about her change of plans, and started to look out suitable clothes for the mountains.

Estella, meantime, sat in her room weeping. She had just arranged to betray the one girl friend she had. "Why, Father," she sobbed, "why have you ordered me to do this?

3

The Gorrats

Deep under the mountain Krask breathed through a handkerchief and looked at the forerunners of his future army. Numbers of the gorrats, shaggy, grotesque looking creatures, prowled about the floor of a large smelly cavern.

Looking small amongst them, a few men in shiny black suits moved about, armed only with a thin rod instrument. "That's called a goad," said Horrold, "it's all you need to control the brutes – but let me demonstrate their obedience."

A slightly smaller creature was sitting against the side of the cave quite peacefully. "He's not as aggressive as we would like – probably a little more intelligent – so we use failures like him to train and test the other gorrats.

"It's a ferocious hybred, a blend of grizzly bear, gorilla and rat. They have all the strength of a gorilla plus the ferocity of a cornered rat with a lot of grizzly bear bad temper. They also breed at a rapid rate – adult in two years. Most important of all they are utterly obedient to our commands. Watch."

One of the men raised his goad. It glowed red and emitted a high pitched piping sound. The creatures all turned to look. The man pointed at the quiet gorrat sitting by himself. "Kill!" he ordered. Immediately the gorrats surged forward in a stampede. Alarmed, the smaller one started to climb up the wall, closely followed by its attackers. Arriving at a ledge some ten metres up, the smaller one started hurling loose rocks down on his foes, dislodging several, while trying to kick the faces of those scrambling onto the ledge.

Eventually his legs were grasped and he was hurled down into the eager claws of those waiting below. In a very little time he was torn to pieces. "Impressive," said Krask, "very impressive, but now I propose another test against a more formidable opponent who is becoming a danger. My spies have been watching him for some time. He is one of the last Ells on Earth"

"A real opponent!" said Horrold with enthusiasm, "splendid!"

Zandor made his way up the long bleak Pyrenean pass. He kept Kuzak to a slow pace as he made regular measurements on an instrument. The readings were interesting; he had entered a zone where Ell bee spies could not operate. The same situation had applied on the other side of the huge mountain on his right. For some reason, someone had something to conceal – and, more worrying, the ability to hide it.

As the day darkened he started looking for a suitable place to camp for the night. Over on his left he saw a waterfall and an area of green near its foot. His Ell senses recognized he was near a Place of Power. Surprised but delighted, he headed towards it. He had a strange feeling of being watched but, though he looked around, he saw nothing to alarm him. He made a brief call to Arlinda but she was still away, so he merely left a message saying that he was near another Place of Power and would call back in a few days.

Far above, from a cave on the opposite mountain, Krask watched through a telescope. Despite the failing light he could see Zandor leading his horse to the water, while a group of fifty gorrats crept towards him through the rocks.

A sharp smell came on the wind. Kuzak lifted his head and whinnied. Zandor swung up into the saddle and raised his staff. Through the gloom he saw a semi-circle of large hairy creatures approaching. He retreated to put the cliff face at his back.

"Stop," he cried, "Go back." His staff threw out the defence that had captured Draach's men, but to no effect. Saliva drooled from the fearsome fangs coming ever closer. Ferocious growls filled the air and Kuzak danced under him, preparing to use his hoofs. A bolt of fire killed the nearest creature, but the others continued to advance. Zandor killed another two, but the inexorable advance continued. Closer and closer they came, with gleaming eyes and horrible breath steaming from their mouths.

From twenty metres, the creatures charged. Zandor realized he could not destroy any more than three or four before they reached him. He raised his staff for the last time.

Krask cursed the fading light but just managed to see the gorrats pounce on the mounted figure and swarm all over it. He turned to Horrold who crouched beside him. "Most satisfactory," he said, and turned back into the passageway leading into the mountain, Horrold trotting behind him.

"Your next task," Krask instructed, "is to set up more breeding caves for these gorrats. The last Ells will leave soon, then we can operate more openly and build an army of unstoppable soldiers."

4

The Silken Cage

Steadily the three made their way up the ascending road. By afternoon the mist had lifted enough to show glimpses of mountain peaks ahead, with the odd gleam of high meadows among the great trees gracing the slopes above them. For a time this bright respite cheered the three companions and, reaching a small plateau, they stopped to admire the view behind them.

Far below now they could see, through the valley gap, the distant patchwork of the vale`s meadows and the slopes of the foothills beyond. Sunlight leant it a distant glamour, as if it was another world. Ahead, the great mountains awaited.

By late afternoon the mist had closed in again. Shivering, they donned their cloaks, plodding onwards. They passed by the waterfall and Santos`s inn, "We shan`t stop here," Yani said.

At last, as evening came on, they saw lights glimmering ahead. "That must be Pilgrims` Gap. Look for some big gates on the left," said Yani, and almost immediately they loomed up, identified by mossy stone eagles perched on each pedestal, and "Eagleskeep" carved below.

They trotted their tired horses up a steep driveway flanked by pine trees, thick, dark and tall on either side, until they emerged onto a flat grassy plateau. In front of them stood a small castle, built hard against the mountain.

They stopped for a moment. "Are you sure this is the right place, Yani?" Ragore asked.

"There's only one way to find out – let's go on, it`s too chilly to hang about here," and Yani rode forwards. As they approached, two heavy doors, higher than Yani on his horse, swung open, admitting them to an inner courtyard. Two figures emerged from a doorway.

"You are expected, gentlemen," said the tallest. "Bring your horses to our stables, I will then lead you to the mistress. My name is Ordesa, and this is Taco. Welcome to Count Aranda`s castle."

Within minutes they were being led from the stables towards a broad flight of stairs. At the top, a door opened and a dark haired figure stepped out.

"Estella!" exclaimed Yani, leaping up the steps, two at a time.

"No," the lady replied, "I am Zenia, Estella's elder sister."

CHAPTER THIRTEEN

1

Trapped

Lucy felt somewhat uneasy as she entered the long compartment. There were several other occupants, all students going for a climbing trip. Estella, the veteran of many such journeys, smiled.

"You see, Lucy, it's not really scary. We go along a sealed vacuum tube, accelerating to 2000 KPH, then there is little sensation till we start to slow down when the seats swivel round. You must not leave your seat but the journey is fast as we don't stop at Madrid."

Well within the hour they reached Taca where Estella said, "Simple, wasn't it? Now there's a link from here to Pilgrims' Gap but it's much slower, half an hour for a short trip. No vacuum tube on this line. Still it's a full day's ride on the surface."

A small electric train provided the transport and they got a compartment to themselves. As they trundled north Lucy felt the sense of unease return. "Cheer up," said Estella, "maybe you're not used to tunnels. I have a calming drink in this flask, we'll drink it as we go."

She produced a flask, unscrewed the top, and a sweet smell permeated the air. Filling the cup Estella handed it to Lucy.

"Your need is greater than mine," she smiled, "so drink it first then I'll have some."

Lucy took the cup and sipped at the cordial. It was as delicious as Estella had promised. She felt wonderful......relaxed..... drowsy.....

She woke in a small room, lying on a bed, with something around her neck. Sleepily she felt it then, hearing voices, tried to sit up .A man in a white coat came in and looked at her. "How do you feel?" he asked.

"I don't know, tired, confused,......the train...... where's Estella?." She fell back on the pillow.

"Well, you fainted on the train, so Estella brought you here. She'll see you later once we have examined you thoroughly. We can't have you falling ill first time in the mountains. Just relax and rest." He then gave her a drink that tasted of herbs and again she fell asleep.

Next time she woke up in a larger room, dimly lit, and became aware of another presence. A figure sat in a chair watching her. It stood up and moved towards her and she thought there was something familiar about it.

"I am a friend," said a gentle, female voice, "unlike those that brought you here. I'm sorry to tell you we're prisoners."

"Prisoners?" said Lucy, shocked into full awareness, "Prisoners indeed! That's not possible. I am an Ell and ...."

"So am I. My name is Elaire and I have been held here for ten years." Lucy stared at her in astonishment.

"Elaire? Zandor's daughter, but you're the one we've come to rescue "

"Rescue?" Elaire asked, astonished.

She laid a finger on Lucy's lips counselling silence. She whispered very softly, "These collars we wear inhibit our natural powers. They're linked to special equipment in the ceiling, also someone will be listening to what we say. Put your hands on my temples, I will do likewise and we can communicate by thought."

Ten minutes later Elaire sat back, understanding all that Lucy had conveyed. Best of all, Yani was alive and had found his grandparents. Elaire wanted to shout with joy but instead she put her hands back on Lucy's head. "Say nothing out loud. Now, think of my son, my little Yani. I want to see him through your eyes. How did you meet him? Tell me everything!"

Lucy thought back over everything involving Yani. When she came to Estella, Elaire jumped up, breaking contact.

"What's wrong?"

Elaire stared at Lucy in alarm, then whispered, "She's Krask's daughter!"

"Krask?"

"It's Krask, Count Aranda, who has kept me here—after my husband was killed. Bandits brought me to him and he paid them."

Lucy looked at her in horror. That explained so many things. She reached for Elaire again and explained that the students were going to Estella's father's house to meet Zandor there.

"But what can we do? Our collars will not come off, so we can't use our powers."

Elaire looked thoughtful.

"Perhaps if we, literally, put our heads together we could send a stronger signal? Let's try to concentrate and warn Yani. Something may remain of my link to him.

Not far away Yani, Ragore and Pasco were shown to the three rooms allocated to them by Ordesa. Zenia had invited them to join her for supper at nine o'clock. Yani, lying in a warm bath, suddenly felt as if someone was shouting to him from a great distance. He put his hands over his face, sat up and tried to open his mind. "Lucy?" he wondered, "and someone else," What were they shouting? "Danger! Beware of Estella and Zenia. Take great care."

Disturbed, he dressed hurriedly and went to tell the others. Gathered together in Ragore's room, they looked at each other, then Ragore said carefully, "But your feelings for Estella?" Yani flushed a little but tried to look at their relationship objectively.

"I suppose I made most of the running. I still don't know what she really thinks, but she's—"

"What?"

"Gorgeous," Yani mumbled.

"Hmmmph!" Pasco grunted, "Well let's be careful in what we say and eat and drink. Anyway you may be misled, Lucy's safe in Altania."

Supper was laid out in a dining hall, very welcoming with flagstones on the floor, green velvet curtains drawn and a fire casting a flickering light on the silver candelabra enhancing the oak table. Wine gleamed red in crystal decanters and platters of breads, salads, meats and cheeses were laid out on a side table. Zenia, now wearing a long crimson gown, entered by a side door and lit the candles, while the three friends stood by the fire.

"Up here in the mountains we need a fire to take the chill off the night air."

"It creates a homely atmosphere," remarked Ragore, and received a rare smile from Zenia.

"You are all very welcome here," she said, "now let us drink to our meeting. Father and Estella should be here by tomorrow morning, meanwhile you only have me." She poured wine into four glasses and carried them over to the fire. "To an interesting visit!" she said and, lifting her glass, took a generous mouthful.

Encouraged by this, her guests followed suit and soon were talking quite freely about the journey. They were further relaxed by a fine supper and afterwards responded to Zenia's questions about life in Altania .

She turned her smoky green eyes on Yani. "And what about when all the Ells have departed, what will happen then?"

Yani pursed his lips, "I hope life will continue much as it is. Humankind now has the chance to evolve as the Ells did long ago."

"But what of mankind's selfishness?"

"Ell education teaches self discipline and tolerance."

"Ha! Text-book answer. Tell me do you really believe the Intervention was necessary?"

"Look, Zenia, I experienced 'untaught' man in Polonia. Believe me, Ell teaching is a great improvement."

"How much of humankind do you think agrees with you?"

"Most people benefit hugely from what the Ells did. Even before the Intervention I believe most thinking people saw the abyss ahead of them. Anything was preferable to that."

"I am sure that's right," said Ragore, "once you've given a blind man his sight, does he want to part with it? Earth today is largely a paradise, a blend of natural living and scientific progress. Everyone is taught to use their talents."

Zenia laughed, "The Chinese have a saying—' Why do you hate me? I have never helped you.' Humans are strange creatures, do the Ells really understand them? However don't mind me, I love playing devil's advocate, that's an old phrase you may not know."

"Oh I understand it well enough," said Ragore, "but what do you really think?"

"That will wait for tomorrow, or our next meeting," said Zenia, rising, "It's been an interesting evening for me, we don't have enough visitors."

"We were hoping to meet an old friend here," said Pasco. "An older man, very distinguished. He may have left a message."

"No," said Zenia, "you are the first visitors for several months, but I'll make enquiries in the morning. Now, have a good night's sleep – please ask Ordesa if there is anything you require." She smiled at them and left, suggesting they finish the wine.

An hour later she joined her father, who had watched the proceedings on a relay. "What do you think?" Zenia asked him.

Krask scowled. "I think Yani's the most dangerous. I would say kill him and work on the others, except that I have his mother and with him as a prisoner will be able to exert pressure on her. Also Estella wants him for herself and I need her full cooperation.

"Now go and release enough gas into their rooms to knock them out for twelve hours. Tomorrow we will limit their powers and when they wake they'll be inside the mountain and helpless. You never know, if I can bend them to my service, they would be powerful tools."

Alone in his room Yani felt a great tiredness falling on him. He shook his head to clear it—he must do something. This Bee he had been given, where was it. He closed his eyes and concentrated. At once he had a view of himself from just above. "Go up to the ceiling," he thought, and the view changed.

He opened his eyes and tried in vain to see it. "Damned thing must be tiny, smaller than the Ell bees. I`ll send it through the key hole to find out what this danger is."

Yani sat down and, closing his eyes, concentrated on steering his tiny spy along the corridor and downstairs. "I`m like a ghost!" he thought, "an invisible ghost!"

At last he heard the murmur of voices and overheard Zenia talking to a huge bearded man. "That must be her father," Yani muttered. Listening, he realized the trap they had fallen into. Ragore and Pasco—he had to warn them, they had to leave at once.

It was approaching one o'clock. He had a sudden wish for fresh air and opened the window. Leaning out he saw the ground at least twenty metres below him. His staff had some sort of anti-gravity device—could it hold him? He held it up and felt the pull. Now he had to get Pasco and Ragore! He ran to the door but it had been locked. Even as he examined it, a noise came from above. Gas hissed out of the ventilator. Yani`s head started to spin.

"Don`t breathe," he thought, running back to the window. Fresh mountain air blew in as he leaned out and peered around. The moonlight was bright enough to show the sheer fall below and the plain wall rising up into the sky above.

"We`re in a trap," he muttered to himself. "I`d better stay free for the moment, if this thing will take my weight."

He climbed onto the window ledge then, quivering nervously, held the staff above his head. It seemed to pull upwards, but would it hold him, or was he about to be dashed to pieces on the ground below? It might be safer to let them capture him.

"Never!" he swore, took a tight grip and jumped into space.

"Lift me," he commanded, then the next moment he was hurtling skywards, soaring high into the night sky.

"Not so high!" he yelled, hanging on to this mad instrument. "Slowly downwards, down to the ground," he said in a quieter tone.

At last he realized he was drifting gently to the ground. "Hold tight! Don't let go," he told his aching hands.

At last his feet touched solid earth and he stamped on the ground in relief. He rubbed his hands to get some feeling back and looked round for a path leading upwards.

"Caves," he muttered, "I must find an entrance." If Zenia's father was the enemy, the caves would probably run from behind the castle. Scrambling to his feet he set off up the mountainside, moonlight silvering the ground.

An hour later he came to a cliff face, rearing high above. Ten metres up, a shadow suggested an opening—but how to get up there? Could his staff lift him again? He grabbed it with both hands and thought "Gently, lift!"

Gradually it started to rise till his feet left the ground then it continued to lift him up and up. He hung on with aching arms, frightened to relax his grip till at last he reached the opening he had seen. Thankfully he put his feet onto a ledge of solid rock. A small black hole lay behind. Cautiously Yani squeezed through the gap. Inside blackness swallowed him.

"I need a light and it's in my saddlebag," Yani muttered.

Immediately his staff started to shine and Yani made out a tunnel opening before him. Suddenly shaking with relief, his legs collapsed. "A few minutes rest," he thought, but moments later he was asleep.

Outside, the silver and black hillside lay silent. Shadows lengthened as the moon declined, but nothing else changed till dawn when, from the house far below, the sound of shouting and yells drifted up the mountain. Yani, exhausted, slept on.

Zenia, waking early, had gone to check on her captives. Yani's absence from a locked room without a credible exit, provoked uproar. Both Ragore and Pasco lay senseless in a drugged sleep and were taken to Krask.

"I knew he was dangerous," growled Krask. "He manages to fly from a window twenty metres high or walk through a locked door – we must find him before he does any more damage. I'll set the gorrats on his trail. They can deal with him as they dealt with his grandfather."

"That won't please Estella, she's quite fond of him."

"Estella will have to accept it," Krask growled.

Two hours later twenty gorrats arrived with Horrold's chief handler, a dour man named Swarth. Immediately he set the hideous creatures to work, sniffing the grounds. Within minutes a cry from one of them alerted Swarth.

"Seek!" he shouted, "Seek!" The pack, followed by Swarth, started up the mountain track.

Access to Krask's caverns lay behind the castle's cellars. Ragore and Pasco knew nothing of this, or of their journey into the mountain. The young captives were lodged securely in separate cells by the time they regained consciousness. Krask saw them individually and made the same offer to each of them.

"I am sorry to have brought you here like this, but your companions have left you. You are a highly trained young man but you've been softened by these interlopers called Ells from another world. I offer you a chance, a wonderful chance, to regain your true heritage as a son of Earth, a warrior of power, a prince of your subjects, empowered under me to rule as you please.

"The Ells' time has past and I have an unconquerable army ready to take control, first of this great peninsula, then of adjoining lands to the North and East. Already I am in touch with secret groups spread throughout the Americas and in Asia – nothing is going to stop me expunging the shame of the Intervention! You may join me as my lieutenant whenever you wish – or remain here at my pleasure. Think well – I shall return later!"

Ragore and Pasco both responded in similar ways. Treating Krask's request with contempt, they concentrated on a series of mental exercises designed to heighten their perception, but unusually these had little effect. Something seemed to hinder them and each sensed some form of inhibiting vibration. They turned to physical exercises with more success and eventually tired themselves to the point where they could sleep.

CHAPTER FOURTEEN

River Run

The sound of the hunters woke Yani. He crawled back to the ledge and peered down. A harsh voice floated up to him.

"Good gorrats, seek on, seek on, seek and kill!"

Yani gasped. A group of ferocious bear-like creatures had started to climb up towards him. Hands with long claws gripped the rock face as hungry faces stared up at him, the great jaws slavering in anticipation of blood—his blood!

He squirmed back down the narrow opening leading to the long tunnel. Seizing his staff he set off into the mountain. Behind him, a gorrat, hot on his scent, was trying to squeeze through the entrance. Its baffled roars pursued Yani as he ran. After a time he realized that he could no longer hear it. It must be stuck, unable to get in, and he slowed his pace.

The tunnel exited high up in a mighty cavern. A flight of narrow steps clung to the wall and led down to the distant floor. He noticed two figures entering the cavern at the far end. Yani could see a stairway behind them, presumably leading to a lower level. Yani recognized Zenia and her father, who seemed to be issuing instructions.

Yani released his personal Bee and willed it to fly down. He caught fragments of conversation. "…..the vibration confuses them. Start the drug treatment tomorrow and soon they'll no longer know who they are. In a month, they will be ready for re-training and in two year`s time what great commanders they`ll be!"

"But what about their powers, Father?"

"Ha! There`s a unit in the roof of each cell that numbs and blocks their abilities. Later they`ll be collared. Now I`m off to make sure that Yani is caught and killed."

"Bee," Yani thought, "Fly down that stairway"

He closed his eyes and saw the stairs, then a long line of cells. He spotted Ragore's at one end and Pasco's further along; now he knew where to go. Bringing his bee back to watch the cavern, now empty, he headed for the stairs.

"Ah," he exclaimed. On the stairway, though far down, four gorrats had started to climb up. He had to move quickly. Again he took hold of his staff. He would have to hang on for ages, the floor was far below, but would the shadows hide him? Taking his life in his hands once more, he grabbed his staff tightly and jumped out into space, hoping his momentum would carry him across the cavern to the shadows at the far side.

Drifting down through the gloom, Yani examined the layout. The cavern served as a central hall, with passages running off in all directions. At least the entrance to the stairway and the cells lay near to where he was heading. Slowly the floor came closer till at last, arms aching, he landed and looked around. Apart from the creatures now well up in the gloom, no one seemed to be about.

Running across, he went through the archway and started down some stairs. Unfortunately, at the bottom, a guard appeared, looked up and opened his mouth to shout. Yani jumped forward swinging his staff and knocked the fellow senseless.

Quickly rolling the guard inside the first empty cell, Yani locked him in. Moments later Ragore lifted his head as his door opened. He seemed drugged, staring at Yani without recognition. A numbing vibration came from a device hanging from the ceiling. Lifting his staff, Yani struck it as hard as he could—then mayhem broke out.

A flash like lightning lit the cell, and alarms started to clamour. Yani grabbed Ragore's arm and shook him.

"Follow me, run!" he shouted.

Ragore staggered to his feet, shook his head to clear it and stumbled off down the corridor after Yani, who was opening another cell. Pasco stood clutching his head when Yani burst in.

"Yani! What—?"

"Pasco!" yelled Yani, "follow me," and again he ran off down the corridor. At the same moment a horrific roar came from behind. They swung round then gasped in terror, a gorrat charged down the corridor towards them. Pasco and Ragore threw themselves to one side as Yani raised his staff and a bolt of energy knocked the creature flat.

"Run," Yani shouted and they emerged into a hall with several openings.

"Look, there`s an iron grating to close off this corridor," Ragore said. They grasped it, heaved it across and bolted it. More gorrats appeared at the far end and Yani fired more bolts before the three youngsters retreated into a side tunnel.

At that moment a strange thing happened. The staff in Yani`s hand became three, the original and two of different colours, all emitting light. He handed one each to his friends who, though baffled by this conjuring trick, nevertheless accepted them.

"There`s cold air blowing up, perhaps we can get out this way," Pasco said, running ahead. Down and down they went. Every junction caused a problem. Time after time they had to retrace their steps and each minute they expected more gorrats to rear up out of the darkness. Fortunately none did, but hours passed before they came to a wide cavern with a river running down the middle—and daylight at the far end.

"Down to a sunless sea," murmured Yani, who rather enjoyed raiding Sinclair`s memory for suitable quotations.

"What did you say, Yani?" Pasco asked.

"Nothing, just a bit of poetry."

"It`s a bit of poetry that got us into this," Pasco muttered back at him.

In the main cavern, confusion reigned. Finding the cell passageway littered with dead gorrats, and noting the closed gate at the far end, Krask gave up attempts to get in that way. Baffled by what had happened, he assumed the worst. Somehow his prisoners had regained their powers and escaped. Soon they could be away from the mountains, summoning help that would destroy his caverns and the work of generations. However, there was only one way they could get out.

Krask explained matters to Zenia. "I can catch them at the river exit, and destroy them before they can send any messages.

"However, as a precaution, we shall move immediately to our secret base in Mahoural mountain. Its entrance is well hidden half-way along the road tunnel. We will breed many gorrats – our future army – and wait till all the Ells go. Also we have accumulated bits from old matter transformers and I have ordered the capture of a scientist who will build one for us.

"You and Estella will leave for the east with a strong bodyguard under Solo`s command. He is devoted to you. Also Estella`s child – Yani's child – will become a weapon for the future. Never let it know who its father is for, if by any chance he escapes alive, Yani could become our greatest foe. Use all the knowledge from Estella`s studies, and develop a range of weapons." Krask planned for every foreseeable eventuality, even his own capture or death.

"Wait here for a minute," Yani said, "there`s something I must do." He moved forwards till he was out of sight before sending Bee ahead to reconnoitre. He closed his eyes to watch what the bee relayed back to him. At the side of the water lay a black inflatable raft, probably used for fishing. Beyond it, Yani saw the river flowing out from the mountain and travelling rapidly over the valley floor, before disappearing into a gorge. Unfortunately, the riverbank was lined with gorrats waiting for them.

He sent his bee down the gorge and realized that the raft could probably sail down river for a few kilometres to a jetty. There a path led up to the road. Yani noticed that not far past the jetty the river vanished into a colossal waterfall.

Recalling his bee, Yani returned to the others and told them of the gorrats outside. "But I have found a solution," he said and led them forwards to the raft.

"You mean you just found this too?" asked Ragore.

"It must be Krask`s. D`you think he`d mind if we borrowed it?" This produced a few smiles.

"It`s dark now, and there are black oilskins in the raft. If we put these on and drift down the river we may not be seen."

"Rafts, oil skins, new staffs – Yani, you've become a real wizard!" said Ragore, "How do you do it?"

"I`ll tell you later," Yani promised, "but look at that."

The exit was filled by the river running out, but a strong chain had been rigged up to give access from the outside. Claw over claw a shaggy creature was hauling itself up along the chain. Its gutteral grunts alerted Yani. He ran forward to the entrance, Pasco and Ragore at his heels, and tried to knock it into the water with a bolt from his staff. Twice he missed the swaying target before Ragore tried his staff.

"Ha!" he cried in triumph, as the creature disappeared into the swirling water.

"That was a scout. When it doesn`t return they will know for certain we are here. We should leave at once."

Quietly they settled themselves in the raft. Yani sent his bee on to fly about five metres in front so that he could have some help in guiding the raft. Seized by the current they shot off into the fiercer flow and everyone huddled down, trying to remain unseen.

Cloaked by darkness, they emerged into the open, scarcely daring to breathe. The first minute passed in silence till a shaft of moonlight hit them for a moment; it was enough! A hideous screech that split the air was followed by the splash of bodies leaping into the river.

"They`re coming for us!" Ragore cried. "I can`t aim properly from this raft."

"Wait till they`re closer, you`ll never hit them at this range."

The raft turned and swirled in the current, upsetting their bolts, but their speed left the first gorrats behind. Almost immediately another group further down the river jumped in and started towards the raft. For a moment the raft steadied.

"Firing now," Ragore shouted and his first bolt hit home.

"Got another," Pasco yelled.

Ahead of them they could just make out the heads of gorrats swimming directly into their path. Others had misjudged and turned back but two in particular were right in their path. Their huge claws reached out, their ghastly jaws gaped. "Fire quickly," shouted Ragore but the raft hit a rock, and the bolts went wide. At the last moment Yani struck one between the eyes and it disappeared.

Suddenly the whole raft tilted up. The survivor had gripped the back with one paw. Its foul breath engulfed Ragore, just before he fired straight down its throat. The raft crashed down again as the gorrat fell off.

The dark jaws of the gorge opened to receive them. Down they lurched, acceleration throwing them back as they hurtled into the foaming maelstrom ahead. Yani, conscious of the energy pulsing through his staff, wedged it into two of the safety ropes. He kept his hand on it, closed his eyes and willed the Bee`s sight into the staff.

Like a wild animal the raft came alive beneath them. It bucked and reared, threatening to bounce them into the water. Time and again they were tossed into the air and their knuckles ached as they gripped the safety ropes. Rocks grinned their ragged teeth at them as they flashed by at an alarming pace. The gasps from the passengers went unnoticed, swallowed up in the torrent`s hungry roar. All the time the staff twisted and pulled, guiding them down the best route.

At last the frantic rush slackened and they drifted onto a mini lake, shining under the moon. Over on the right the jetty promised freedom. .

"Yani, you`ve done it, we`ve got away!" Ragore shouted. Yani said nothing, experience had made him wary. He sent Bee over to the jetty then up the path.

"Gorrats!" he cried, fists clenched in disappointment, "the path's full of them. We can't get out that way."

Though the waterfall lay ahead, Yani knew he had to think of a solution. "We must go on further. Wedge your staffs under the safety ropes like mine— then hold on tightly," he ordered. "Be quick!" Seconds later the current grabbed the raft, hurling it into the lower gorge at breakneck speed, swirling and turning as the currents again took hold. Water cascaded around, leaping into the air and soaking them. It became impossible to speak and increasingly difficult to stay in the boat as it bumped, twisted and threatened to overturn.

A vast plume of spray ahead, coupled with a growing thunderous roar, promised the advent of the waterfall. "Hold on, hold on," Yani yelled.

All three grabbed the safety ropes as they were swept to the brink – then over and down, down into the dark, falling…..falling…. moonlight and hope vanishing behind them.

***

It was Swarth who brought the news to Krask. "All of them, over the falls?

Better dead than loose, and surely they had no time to send out messages. Well, I'll have to find some other young men with Ell blood to train … that lot would have been difficult anyway. Now back to the caverns. We will close the castle and move to Mahoural's caves, in case any news of our activities here has leaked out. Afterwards my daughters can go to set up operations in the east."

The massive head turned and looked south. "Gone", Krask cried, lifting up his arms, "Drowned Ells! I shall triumph when the rest go – and may they go soon!"

Swarth stood before his master, caught in a mixture of fear, admiration and ambition. Perhaps he could become a senior commander in the new army……

"Don't stand there gawping, Swarth. You've done well, driven them to their doom, but there is still much to do. Call in the gorrats and take them over to Mahoural. I`ll join you in a few days."

***

Down, down and down they fell, through the maelstrom of mist and spray, thundering up from the rocks below.

Yani was the first to become aware that they were not only falling but gliding forward and heading towards the deep, clear waters beyond the rocks. He sensed the energy coursing through all the staves wedged through the ropes. At last they crashed down onto the water with enough force to shake them, but in a gentler manner than they had feared. "Wow!" said Pasco, "How did we do that?"

For another hour they continued to hurtle down the river guided by the bee in front, leaping obstacles, boulders and smaller waterfalls, though not able to see much in the dark canyon. Occasionally a gleam of moonlight would catch a foaming crest of water flashing past, then it was gone, but the roar of the angry water drowned any attempt to speak. Not until the speed of their headlong rush began to lessen as the canyon walls fell away, did anyone try to say anything.

Typically it was Pasco, breathless with excitement, "I don`t suppose we could go back and do that again?"

Ragore, who felt he`d forgotten how to breathe, uttered a strangled threat to throw Pasco overboard if he ever made such a suggestion again, and Yani laughed.

"We need somewhere to rest," Pasco said after a little while.

"I`m thinking," Yani replied, then lapsed into silence as the river carried them rapidly downstream. The cliffs fell away as they glided into a wide valley. Fields and trees opened on either hand and the river sound was quietening. A town slid quietly past; "That`s Taca," said Pasco. Soon it was far behind as they drifted on through the night. Silence surrounded the raft, while the light of the moon spun a magic world of silver and shadows to soothe them after the terrors of the gorge.

Yani bent forward and pressed his forehead against his staff. He still sensed the energy coursing through it and the other staves, guiding them safely as Bee`s vision linked into the staff via the implant in his head. Where were they headed?

In response to his thought, Bee soared up, higher and higher, till Yani could glimpse a moon-lit lake, with a long wooded island, lying far ahead. He looked back at the others.

"We are all tired," he said, "By dawn we should have reached safety, but till then you should rest." He spoke with such certainty that no one argued. Making themselves as comfortable as possible, they sank into a half sleep, lulled by the dreamlike meadows and trees drifting by. Gently the river carried them now, whispering water tales as they travelled. The sky above was full of stars, dimmed only by the moon riding high above. Now and then the odd hoot of a hunting owl broke the silence of the woods and so, trusting his bee and staff to guide them, Yani slept.

At last the stars paled and a slight flush rose in the east. Yani woke first and, looking back, saw the mountain peaks in the north behind them beginning to glow. He turned and realized they had drifted into a large lake, while straight ahead lay an island. The water was still, like mercury, reflecting only the faint colours of the lightening sky and the dark shadow of the trees ahead.

The raft touched the shore so lightly that none of his companions woke. Yani stepped out and tethered the bow rope to a tree at the water`s edge. A path took him upwards and through a stand of young birch trees. Coming to the edge of a small meadow he saw, facing him, a long, two storied manor house with turrets at either end. Built of grey stone, it had a quiet welcoming air, while the smoke rising from one chimney indicated that someone was awake early! Somehow it seemed familiar, though he couldn`t think why.

Yani made his way back to the raft where he found Pasco had woken and, concerned to find Yani gone, had then roused Ragore. "No need for alarm," said Yani, "here we are safe and, I think, in time for breakfast."

"Now that would be your best trick yet," remarked Ragore. "Breakfast in the middle of nowhere! When did we last eat?"

"Come," said Yani and reached out his hand to help his friends out of the raft. He brought them along the path.

"What a charming house," said Pasco as they caught sight of it, "Do you think they will welcome us?"

"I believe so – let's find out," and again Yani led them forwards. The pathway bore left to circle the manor and then to the main door facing south. As they came round the eastern turret the rising sun fired the autumn colours in the chestnut, maple and oak trees guarding the far side of the lawn. Birdcalls echoed back and forth in the fresh morning air. The front doors opened and a familiar figure stepped out, arms spread, calling, "Welcome! Welcome to Marmorian!"

"Salvador!" exclaimed Yani, who had guessed correctly. "I had hoped this would be the island you told me about."

"Yani!" Salvador exclaimed, "and Pasco and...?"

"This is Ragore, the one who broke his arm."

"I am delighted to see you three, but where's Zandor. Arlinda called me to say you had gone off to join Zandor. I've been half expecting you to make your way here."

"Grandpa has disappeared somewhere in the mountains. It's a long story—"

"Later," said Salvador, "Before anything else is said, come in, refresh yourselves and then we will have breakfast together. Upstairs there are rooms – and baths – for each of you, also plenty of clean clothes. Here you are completely safe, so lay your worries aside. Later we will talk about everything!"

Inside, a panelled hall displayed a curved open staircase leading to a gallery. Upstairs wide corridors led to the east and west wings, and Salvador, going before them, showed each of them to their rooms. "I have cousins, Jon and Alma, who retired from running a wayhouse to stay here and look after me. Its so quiet here that they are happiest when I have guests, so you are doubly welcome."

CHAPTER FIFTEEN

1

Marmorian

After breakfast, Yani, aided by Ragore's interjections, related their adventures.

"Well," Salvador responded, "at least you seem to have identified your enemy, but I think you should tell Zandor before planning an attack. By the way, I may have found some interesting information. Remember Peter?"

"Who could forget him," Yani laughed.

"Well, apparently he was sent to stay with his uncle three years ago after his parents were killed in the mountains by some wild beasts. They were instructors at the winter sports place up on Mahoural mountain—that's further up the valley from where you were, and on the other side. Peter told me that his parents had found a cave near their home, and seemed concerned about something inside. They closed it off, but two days later their bodies, horribly mutilated, turned up on the valley floor."

Pasco whistled, "Gorrats—or an early version."

"Somebody is trying to hide something, it seems to me," Yani mused. "If that other mountain contains Krask's main base, Mother must be there." He jumped up and started pacing round the room. "Where is little Peter?"

"Right behind you," giggled a small voice, and Yani spun round.

He blinked. Before him stood a clean, well dressed child; only the cheeky face was familiar. Peter looked anxiously at Salvador, "Is it all right to come in now?" he asked. "You said after breakfast."

"Of course it is," Salvador replied. "I'm sure Yani would like to know more about these caves your Dad found."

Peter's eyes sparkled. "It's a bit difficult. I'm sure I would remember if you took me there—"

"No way!" Salvador said quickly, "Janine would skin me alive when she returns."

"But if we just flew up, I could point out where and—"

"Peter!"

Yani saw the determined look in the little fellow's eyes and spoke quickly. "Leave that for now, tell me where is Janine?"

"She's gone off to Madrid for a month and left Peter here. We've been doing some riding and sailing on the lake—"

"And fishing," Peter chipped in. "You should see Salvador handle a rod."

"Well that's fine," said Yani, "but how do we find Zandor? That must be the first thing,"

"When he didn't make his promised call to Arlinda yesterday, she became concerned and called me. She's returning to Altania immediately. When I give her your news, I think she'll fly straight up here."

"Let's call her now," Yani suggested.

Three hours later a flyer arrived, and Arlinda stepped out. "I brought the ten seater. I thought we might need it. Turias sends his regards, by the way. Now, where's our host?"

"He's taken Peter fishing. He thought we should be left in peace to make our plans."

"This is very disturbing," Arlinda said, after the students had given her a graphic description of the gorrats. "If he met a lot of these creatures they could have overwhelmed him." She thought for a bit, then continued. "His last message did mention a Place of Power—that could account for his silence."

"What's a Place of Power?"

"I will show you later. First we should retrace his footsteps. Ells are more difficult to kill than you can imagine and I've an idea how to find him. We'll come to that later, after you explain how you saved your friends from the waterfall."

Everyone looked expectantly at Yani. His blue eyes gazed round them thoughtfully then, holding it out, he told the story of his new staff. This was beyond Ell technology, something ancient, a gift of the Elders perhaps; no one spoke for some time.

Ragore broke the silence. "You mean that thing's alive?" he growled.

"Not exactly, but it has some artificial intelligence and a powerful anti-gravity device."

Ragore shook his head in disbelief.

"Well," said Yani, "Pick up the staff I gave you. Hold it horizontally with both hands and tell it, think it, to lift you two metres off the ground."

"Yani – if this is your idea of a joke, staff or no staff, I'll chuck you in the river!" Nevertheless, though very self-consciously, Ragore stood and held his staff level with the ground and above his head.

"Command it," said Yani, while they all watched.

Slowly it became apparent that Ragore was struggling to hold on to his staff as it started to rise. When his head was about to bump the ceiling they heard him say –   "Down, down, but slowly!" and down he came, to stand flushed and astonished, on the floor.

He smiled sheepishly. "All right, Yani, I'm convinced. So that's how we escaped, the staffs lifted the raft."

Arlinda said "There's something else I must tell you. Pasco, apparently your sister travelled north with Estella last week. I only found out when I tried to contact her this morning."

Pasco's face went white. "Oh no," he whispered. "That means she'll be a prisoner too." He covered his face with his hands.

"Now we've three reasons to go back quickly," Arlinda said

"You mean, back to Krask's valley?" Ragore asked.

"Exactly! This time we'll be prepared."

"And this time," Yani said, suppressed fury in his voice, "We will destroy his equipment, his gorrats, his—"

"His daughters?" Ragore questioned, and Yani stopped. No one spoke for a moment, then he lifted his head, looking confused.

"Oh, I don't know. Estella misled me, but…but.."

149

"But what, my boy?" Arlinda asked gently.

"I still think she really likes me," he muttered.

"Then we'll need to see if we can convert her, but first of all we must plan!" said his grandmother. She looked up as Salvador returned, minus Peter, who had gone to help Jon put their gear away.

"Salvador, you've been so kind to us all, I really don't know how to—"

"Nonsense, I'm delighted to help. Have you decided what to do?"

Ragore said, "Pasco and I should use our new staffs in real action – so far all we've done is run away!"

"Very wise under the circumstances," remarked Salvador. "Now may I suggest that you practice with your staffs first before setting off. May I recommend you design a strong back harness to sheath them so that you needn't have to hold on with your hands when you need to be lifted. Also, I've a lifetime's experience of these mountains and would like to go over the maps with you in detail."

Yani and his companions spent a couple of days on Salvador's island, Marmorian. The autumn evenings were still warm and the night sky full of stars as the good weather continued. They walked back and forth on the forest tracks – the island was over four kilometres long—discussing possibilities. Strangely Arlinda seemed quite relaxed about Zandor's silence. Also she kept glancing at Yani's staff and frowning as if trying to remember something.

"I have an idea what's happened," she said. "Leave it for now. By the way, that little chap Peter is quite a character."

"Salvador and Janine are a good influence. He's quite fearless and wants to show us this entrance."

Arlinda shrugged. "We can look after him. I think we may need him to show us where to get in. It's a big area to search without help."

"When do the autumn storms begin?" asked Yani, as he stood with Salvador looking wistfully at the full glory of the chestnut, oak, beech and maple trees glowing in the sun. "It seems a pity that all this will be blown away."

"Soon the first snows will come to the peaks and high valleys – you should not try to search through the winter, so aim to be back here by mid November. After that, everything will be covered and the only way to travel will be to fly. I'll stock up so that you can all winter here if necessary."

"Well then, we'd better leave in the morning," said Yani, and went to find the others. "Grandma can pilot us up," he told them. "Remember we left our horses at the castle so with luck we can ride them back to Taca."

Very early next morning, as they prepared to leave, Salvador came out to the lawn to wish them good luck. Arlinda thanked him again for his hospitality and added,

"Don't worry! We shall be careful, but the first thing is to find Zandor."

Rising into the brightening skies, Yani and his companions were entranced by the panorama opening before them. Far beneath the river wandered through the plain in great sweeps and bends. The trees scattered glowing carpets of gold among the green of the meadows, and here and there they could make out the regular pattern and grey walls of a farm or small village. Ahead, and rising to meet them, lay the great mountains, stretching east and west as far as they could see.

"How will we ever find Zandor in there?" Ragore called to Yani.

"Well, we know he was somewhere beyond Pilgrims' Gap. He had narrowed his search down to that area."

They flew on, the mountains loomed higher and, following the river up its valley, well before midday they caught site of the cataract.

"Round the hill, there is Pilgrims' Gap – and Krask's castle. There must be an entrance to the caverns from there," cried Pasco.

"Wait," said Yani, "we still have the benefit of surprise. Don't waste it," and he sent a bee down to reconnoitre. Despite a careful search, no sign of life was to be found.

151

"Our horses, where are they?"

"Look nearer the castle – there are three horses in a field and they look familiar."

"First let's check the caverns. Grandma, can you land us near that ledge," and Yani pointed to the place he had hidden after his escape from the castle. Expertly Arlinda brought them to land and they climbed out.

"I'll send my bee down into the mountain, so there's no need for us to go in yet."

"I thought our spy-bees can't operate here," Arlinda said.

Yani looked smug. "But mine can, it came with the staff and all I have to do is close my eyes and will it to move. Mind you, it can only go a few kilometres from me."

"That staff of yours is a strange thing, Yani."

They all sat still while Yani sent his bee on its way. A thorough search proved that the whole complex seemed empty and had the appearance of a place abandoned in a hurry.

"It's absolutely empty," Yani said at last, "nothing there at all."

"They must have gone somewhere," grumbled Ragore, disappointed that he couldn't get to grips with his captors.

The mountainside was deserted. They took to the air again and flew up and down the valley but saw no sign of life.

"These creatures were real," said Yani, "and Krask is a very dangerous man – and a cautious one. Even though he believed us drowned, we might have sent out a message beforehand, so he's gone into hiding. The question is—where?"

"He's only had a little time. There must still be some trace of their route if we can search the ground carefully. I used to go tracking with my uncle when I was small and I haven"t forgotten how," said Pasco.

"And if – when—we are seen, it will draw them out and then we can deal with them. The more ordinary we seem, the more confident Krask will be. He mustn't guess how powerful our new staffs are, so we should go down the mountain, reclaim our horses and ride to Pilgrims' Gap. Krask will be bound to have spies around and word will get to him of Ells in the area—that should draw him out."

"Won't he be surprised," chuckled Ragore.

"But he won't send these gorrats into the village", said Arlinda, "we'll need to go up the pass to offer him a tempting target."

"Grandma, would you please fly us back to that field where we saw the horses. We'll go into the village and try to find if Grandpa passed through and where he was headed. We'll meet you at the inn."

"I'll park the flyer there and hire a horse, then we can search on the ground."

The castle had been abandoned, so Arlinda left them to collect their horses and tack and she went ahead to make her own arrangements. Within the hour they rode up to the village inn where, at Arlinda's insistence, rooms had been booked.

CHAPTER SIXTEEN

1

The High Pyrenees

That evening, Arlinda and Yani made enquiries. They heard of an older man on a big horse who had passed through, going north, about two weeks earlier. He had enquired about a suitable camping site further up the valley, then left the village about midday. No more had been heard of him and travellers coming south had not seen him on the road.

"He was a very distinguished gentleman – not someone you"d forget in a hurry," Juan, the innkeeper, added. At last, some news. Yani was excited – and worried. What had caused Zandor to disappear? Arlinda dropped no hints about what she had in mind.

They left at first light, and soon were urging their horses up the ever-climbing slope, only too aware that Krask might be preparing to attack them. However, the morning passed quietly, the only sign of a problem being the gathering of clouds round the mountain peaks. Here, the winter snows could arrive early.

The skies were darkening by the time they reached the sidetrack which lead to the camping site. They could just see a waterfall with an inviting patch of green on its left. Riding forward, they came to a meadow with a curious statue on the far side near the cliff.

"It's a man on a horse!" exclaimed Pasco, whose eyes were the keenest. They galloped through the grass and reined up around the statue. "It's Zandor!" exclaimed Yani, "on Kuzak – I'd know him anywhere – and Zandor`s got his staff raised."

"Stand back, Yani," Arlinda ordered. She rode up to the statue and laid her staff on it. At first nothing seemed to happen, then the texture of the stone started to shimmer and change – then move!

Zandor`s voice spoke: "Arlinda—I hoped you would guess. Have you seen any monsters? They were overwhelming me and I had to transform and hope—."

"You`ve lost track of time. What happened?"

"I tried to get through to Ellshome but I must have been too far from the centre of the portal and got stuck in limbo. Also, I kept hold of my staff."

"At your age—an elementary mistake my dear husband!"

"With gorrats about to tear me to bits? I think I did rather well. What date is it now?"

"The seventh of October," said Yani, who had been trying to make sense of all this. "What happened to you, Grandpa?"

"I`ll explain later. Right now we need to get back to Pilgrims` Gap. Look at the sky—we`re in for a blizzard." Just as Zandor spoke, small flakes started drifting down.

They set off back down the road but within minutes could hardly see beyond their horses. "Keep bunched together, we mustn`t get separated in this. It can snow for days up here."

The swirling snow made it difficult to concentrate. Cold crept through their clothing as they plodded forwards, trying to stay on the road.

Suddenly a great figure loomed up in front of them, claws reaching out, and instinctively Yani raised his staff and blasted it with flame. It fell to the side but others leapt forward. By now all the staffs were up and a further barrage of fire from Yani, Pasco and Ragore destroyed the creatures instantaneously.

Zandor turned in his saddle. "These are different staffs," he shouted into the wind. "Where did they come from?"

Yani looked from side to side for more gorrats but none appeared. He grinned, "I`ll tell you later, Grandpa, when we exchange secrets."

Cold crawled into their very bones as the wind moaned around them. "Will I ever be warm again?" Yani wondered. Freezing minute followed freezing minute as they plodded down the mountain pass. At last, a good hour later, dark shadows looming on either side showed they had reached

Pilgrims' Gap. The streets were deserted and the houses shuttered against the storm; even the inn was silent. They tethered their horses, staggered up the steps and were thankful to find the door not yet locked.

They found Juan stoking a large fire in the main room. Though surprised by guests arriving in the middle of a blizzard, he shouted for his boy to stable the horses and his wife to open and heat rooms. He then departed to the kitchen, promising to produce a hot meal for his frozen and famished guests "in just a few minutes."

No other travellers came in that evening so, after eating, the five sat round the table discussing plans to rescue the prisoners. The youngsters told Zandor about their adventures and the new staffs but their questions about Places of Power just got the reply, "Later, dear lads, later. We'll show you everything, but not now."

"I've discovered that our bees don't work up in that valley. Krask has some device that hinders them."

"But I have a different type of bee that came with the staff. It doesn't go very far but it operated in the caverns."

"Really?" Zandor looked hard at his grandson, so full of surprises, and held out his hand. "Let me see that staff of yours, Yani." Yani handed it over and Zandor examined it closely. After a long while he spoke.

"This is quite extraordinary, Yani. It is unimaginably old, perhaps made by the Arraqail, a race vanished long before even the time of the Ells. Now and again we find signs of their genius—we suspect that they had something to do with these Places of Power—but no civilization, no building, no remnant of any kind on any world has ever been found. All we have heard has come from ancient legends—and one was about a staff with strange powers. Perhaps—." He stopped and held the staff to his head.

Yani watched closely. Zandor's eyes closed and he seemed to be receiving a message. He nodded as if in agreement then handed it back.

156

"Yes, it`s way beyond our technology and enormously powerful. I also got the impression of a number of staffs coloured like a rainbow. At the moment it`s attuned to you but never let it fall into the wrong hands. How the Elders came by it I`ve no idea, but they are certainly doing their best to help you.

"Now we must find out what`s inside that mountain, where Elaire and Lucy are, and get them out before we attack. With these new staffs even lots of gorrats shouldn`t pose too great a danger."

Pasco spoke. "Remember little Peter?"

Zandor head turned. "Vividly. Why?"

"Apparently his parents lived at the winter sports place half-way up the mountain. They found some entrance that Peter knows about. Possibly they were killed because of what they knew. Apparently they were killed by what sounds like gorrats. Anyway Peter`s offered to show Yani where the entrance is."

"Involving a child—I don`t like it." Zandor snapped.

"But if we fly him up there and he only has to point out the entrance to Yani, he will be safe enough. He can stay in the flyer all the time," Arlinda pointed out. "If we call Salvador we could collect Peter as soon as this blizzard lifts. Also we will need a base up near Mahoural mountain. Perhaps Juan can suggest something."

"See if you can find him, Yani. Ask him to join us for a moment."

Juan, rescued from clearing up in the kitchen, was most helpful.

"Senor, of course. Nothing easier—I own a building beside the lake which lies at the foot of the Mahoural slopes. It`s used as a restaurant, mainly in summer, but when the winter sports start in February I do lunches there. At the moment it`s empty and you may hire it, but I`ve no people to help you."

"We can care for ourselves, Juan. We`ll fly up and take plenty of food but I would not like to advertise our presence."

"There is a big shed where everything is stored. It'll take your flyer with ease. Let me give you the keys and a plan of the place. Tell me what provisions you'll require."

Yani, Ragore and Pasco shared a big room in Juan's inn. At last they were about to act and it took them some time to settle down. The wind howled round the eaves, sounding like gorrats hunting for their prey, but a tiled stove kept them warm.

"How long do these storms usually last, my mountain lad?" Ragore asked Pasco.

"It could snow for a week at this time of year."

"That'll give me time to thaw out my bones, No more winter riding for me! In future I'll fly. Goodnight," and Ragore turned over and went to sleep. Yani lay awake, thinking that perhaps this week he would find his mother...soon...soon.

Two days later the skies cleared and Arlinda flew to fetch Peter, returning within three hours. Salvador had kitted Peter out in winter sports clothes and the boy sparkled with excitement as he ran into the inn, snow scattering from his boots. Arlinda had told him they would fly up to his old home.

"I bet I can remember how to steer a toboggan," he announced. "We could have a race and—."

"Peter, this is not a holiday. You are just going to show Yani where this entrance is but then you must stay in the flyer with Pasco."

"Not even one run?" the child pleaded.

"The runs won't be open yet. It's too soon, but if all goes well you might come back in February," and with this Peter had to be content.

They loaded the flyer with provisions, said farewell to Juan, and flew off to the upper lake. Despite drifting, the building was easily spotted. While snow had piled against the north side, the front remained clear. Yani and Pasco opened the barn doors and Arlinda floated the flyer inside. Ragore departed to start the furnace while the others carted all their goods inside. The ground floor was one large room that served as a restaurant once the season started.

158

Zandor sat down at one of the many pine tables, opened his V-phone, called Madrid and asked for Captain Martinelli. He explained what they were planning to do, adding, `There will be a lot of clearing up once we have the situation under control. If all goes well we should be calling for your help in two or three days."

"Who`s Martinelli?" Yani asked.

"He`s in charge of the emergency services in Madrid."

Zandor turned to Yani. "You've got the hard part to do, I`m sorry to say. With your bee you must explore the layout—once Peter has shown you the secret entrance. We need to get Lucy and your mother out before we attack. We don`t know where the main entrance is, so find that out too, if you can. We don`t want anyone escaping to hide somewhere else."

"It`s still afternoon," Yani said. "If Pasco flies Peter and me up now I can get started. I`ll have a V-phone with me and can report what I find."

Ragore nodded. "That`s fine. Take some provisions with you. Also, since your staff and the ones you gave Pasco and me are the best against the gorrats, one of us should always be with Zandor and Arlinda."

"That`s sensible, Ragore. You stay with my grandparents at all times. Peter, Pasco, let`s go."

The afternoon skies remained clear as they flew up the mountain. "Look," said Peter, "there`s my old home, just behind the lift station." His face tightened as memories flooded back.

Yani put a hand on the child`s shoulder to comfort him. "We`ll do our best to get rid of these nasty creatures, Peter, and it`s very brave of you to help." Peter turned and looked at Yani, his eyes bright with unshed tears. "Yes," he said, "get rid of them."

A fierce cold bit into them as they climbed out of the craft. "The way in is beyond these boulders on the hill behind the house," Peter pointed. "I know my Dad put a door on it before…before," and his voice failed.

"Right," Yani said, "It`s too cold to wait in the flyer. We`ll settle you in the house, put on the heating, then Pasco and I`ll take a quick look."

"But—."

"No buts Peter, please be sensible. Do you want to be a gorrat`s supper?"

"All right, I`ll stay in the house."

The boulders lay below a small cliff. "See," Pasco pointed, "There`s an iron gate bolted to the bottom of the cliff."

"And it`s padlocked. Let me try my staff," and Yani shot a bolt at the padlock.

It shattered and the gate creaked open; beyond gaped a dark, menacing apperature. "Now for my bee," and Yani sat down at the entrance, closed his eyes and sent his bee down into the dark.

While Yani`s bee searched, Pasco stood beside him, watching for any signs of danger and swinging his arms to keep warm. At last Yani opened his eyes and stood up.

"We might be in luck," he said. "It looks as if this is a natural fault but it leads into a lighted corridor with several empty cells. Further on there`s a bigger cell and I could see Lucy sleeping inside. Let me go down and get her, then you can fly both her and Peter down to the lakehouse while I search further for Mother."

"I`ll come down with you and bring Lucy back, it`ll be quicker."

The two scrambled down into the dark, using their staffs to give some light, till they reached the lit passage way.

"I can hear voices," whispered Pasco.

"There`s a side passage, there are men in there."

"Now if they all fell asleep...do you remember that exercise Arlinda taught us?"

Pasco nodded. They pointed their staffs down the passageway and a gentle soothing sound, barely audible, floated away from them.

"That should do it," said Yani, after two minutes, "Let`s check these rooms."

160

The passage led to a number of rest rooms and one larger one.

"It`s where the guards eat," Pasco said, stating the obvious, for around a table, slumped into the remains of a meal, eight burly guards lay fast asleep.

"Now we can send them deeper so they won`t waken for a day," Yani said, and again they used their staffs, till all the guards were snoring. Nevertheless, Pasco locked the door as they left.

Back in the main corridor all remained quiet. Yani pointed, "That`s Lucy`s cell there." Peering through the cell`s window they could see Lucy lying on a bench. She didn`t move as they entered, then Pasco`s shaking voice said "Lucy?"

Slowly her head turned and a pair of dull eyes regarded them suspiciously.

"Lucy, it`s me and Yani. We`ve come to take you home."

Lucy peered at them. She mumbled, "Pasco? Yani? But Krask said you`re dead."

"She`s been drugged," Pasco said. "I`ll take that collar off," and ignoring Lucy`s protests, undid the device around her neck.

"No, no," Lucy sobbed, then cried as a needle, hidden in the collar, jabbed her.

"Take her out, Pasco and I`ll check the other cells for Mother."

Pasco put a comforting arm round Lucy`s shoulders. "Come with me, little sister. You`re safe now, I`ll look after you."

"Good luck, Yani," he added, then turned and coaxed his bemused sister back up the corridor. He had just managed to get Lucy to the exit when she collapsed completely.

"You`re free now, Lucy," he said, kneeling down, but she shook her head.

"Poison," she mumbled. "Mustn`t take collar off without special key. It jabbed me. `Bye, Pasco," and her voice tailed off.

Pasco shouted, "No, Lucy, no. Don`t leave me. Damn it, we`ve just got you back."

He picked her up and carried her down to the flyer. Peter came up from the house. He looked at Lucy and shook his head.

"Get her to Arlinda," he suggested. "Fly her down and I`ll stay and tell Yani what`s happened."

Pasco stared at Lucy. She was unconscious but still breathing. "Right," he said. Heart still thumping, he lifted her into the flyer. "Peter," he said, "stay inside the house till Yani comes back. Tell him I`ll be back for you, but I might be some time." He jumped into the flyer and took off down the mountain.

Minutes later, Arlinda examined Lucy. "This is serious. We must get her to hospital at once. Taca`s the nearest. You`ll want to come, Pasco and then stay with her. I`ll bring the flyer back."

White faced, Pasco could only nod to Zandor and Ragore as he climbed back into the flyer.

Night fell. Zandor paced the floor, looked up the mountain and constantly checked for any sign of the flyer returning. He told himself that Peter should be safe enough in the house, but why had Yani not called, or answered his calls. Ragore sat slumped in a chair, eyes closed, willing Lucy to recover. The diabolical trick of hiding poison in the collar filled him with fury, then he wrenched his thoughts back to Lucy. There was a girl full of fun and courage, a fine sailor, a…she must get better. His fists clenched; he, Ragore, would deal with Krask later.

The hours crawled, morning came, yet still there was no sign of the flyer.

"Whatever has happened?" he asked Zandor, who shook his head.

"Waiting is the most difficult thing to do," he said. "Try hard to think positive thoughts."

Ragore snorted and slumped down in the chair where he had spent the night. Positive thoughts indeed, when—Zandor`s

162

shout broke his reverie. "There it is." They rushed out to watch as Arlinda landed the flyer. She was alone.

"How is Lucy?" Ragore spoke first.

"They stabilized her at Taca but the antidote was in Madrid. That`s why I was so long, we had to fly on there, then wait for results. Pasco has stayed with her."

"Thank heavens she`s out of danger," Zandor said. "Tell us more as we fly up to get Peter, Yani and, let us pray, Elaire. They`ve been stuck up there all night."

All three tumbled into the flyer and they flew straight to the sports station. Ragore jumped out first calling "Peter, Yani," as he made his way to the house.

Silence greeted him. He ran inside, then all through the house, calling ceaselessly. At last he emerged, "There`s no one here," he said, then he saw little footprints going from the house up to a cliff face behind.

"There`s the entrance," Ragore called to the two Ells climbing up behind him. "Peter`s gone in too, but hasn`t come out. No one else has come out either."

"I knew we shouldn`t have brought him," cried Zandor. "That child never does what he`s told. Salvador will never forgive us."

CHAPTER SEVENTEEN

1

The Killing Pit

After Pasco had gone, Yani sent his bee to explore further. At last it came to his mother's quarters guarded by a heavy plate-glass door. Unlike Lucy's cell, they were a suite of comfortable rooms. Elaire stood in front of an easel, painting. Yani caught his breath as, at last, he saw her in person. Unlike Zandor's old pictures her face was etched with sadness and her eyes spoke of a long sorrow.

There was no sign of a guard but the door opened only from the outside. Recalling his bee, Yani ran down the passageway then came to a halt outside the door. What would he say? He took a deep breath and opened the door wide.

"Mother?" he croaked, then cleared his throat and spoke louder, "Mother."

Startled, Elaire turned. She gazed at the figure standing in the doorway.

"Mother...Mother it's me...Yani." He could say no more, but dropped his staff and opened his arms. Slowly, unbelievingly, she took faltering steps towards this apparition...then her arms were around him, pulling him closer and closer into an embrace that was real and no vision, utter bliss to them both.

"Yani, oh Yani," she sobbed, "is it...is it really you? I have dreamed of this moment so long," her words died, but the blessed sound of her voice filled his heart till he felt it must burst. Coiled together, oblivious of their surroundings, they simply held each other in an embrace that banished the years.

Frail beneath his hands, slimmed by years of captivity, this was still the Mother he remembered. She stepped back a little, her hands now light on his shoulder, and her eyes, tremulous with tears, devoured him.

"Oh, Yani my son, my boy, let me look at you." Her head shook slowly with wonder and tears spilled tracks of joy down her face. "You're so tall... oh the years, all the years I've missed." Her hands, feather-light, wandered down his arms till they reached his own, which she seized in a fierce grip. "All these years, praying, hoping without hope knowing I was presumed dead...then Lucy came and I knew that somehow, somehow you would come."

"You have been with me every single moment," he murmured, then blushed as he remembered Estella.

"Every night I tried to reach you despite this damnable collar. I didn't know if you could hear me. I sent in hope."

"Oh I heard you, every night, and I learned from my dream lady, but I didn't know who you were—not till Grandma told me. But now we must get out of this place."

"I daren't undo this collar without Krask's key. There's a poisoned needle inside."

"Lucy!" Yani cried, "we took her collar off. But Grandpa will have a solution and he's waiting down the mountain. Come on, I'll protect you meanwhile," and he picked up his staff.

They made for the door, then a cloud of gas from the ceiling enveloped them. Yani fell forward into the corridor, gasping for breath. His last thought was to hide his staff. He flung it up the corridor with the command, "Get out!," then everything went dark.

Yani recovered consciousness slowly. He tried to move his arms but found they were held at the wrists by iron cuffs. He lay, spreadeagled on his back, facing a locked door. After a while this opened and two men came in.

"Feeling a little better, are we?" one sneered, lifting a foot to kick Yani.

"No, Cob, better not. He needs to be in good shape to fight, not that it'll make much difference," and the speaker laughed hoarsely.

Memory came back. He had just found his mother, then the gas had come down. His staff—where was his staff?

"How are you going to feed him, Jem?" Cob asked.

"Loosen the ropes a little."

Perhaps, Yani thought, this would give him a chance to break free. However Cob only gave him enough slack to lift his head and drink from the soup-cup Jem held. Afterwards they left him and locked the door. The hot liquid churned in his stomach and his mouth felt foul.

"It`s the remains of the gas. Must keep the soup down, need my strength...now pull yourself together," he told himself. He noted the V-phone had gone from his belt.

"Bee," Yani thought, "Out into the corridor," He flew the bee to the limits of its range but found nothing but empty passages. He remembered his last instruction to Pasco.

"Get Lucy to Arlinda and then fly back. We`ll wait for you at the lift station house."

Now everything was in disarray. He blamed himself, he should have expected the door to be alarmed. Now Mother was not free and he had failed. He tugged at his cuffs but neither they nor the rope would give way. "Be patient," he told himself.

The night passed before the door creaked open and the men returned. Each undid a rope from the wall rings but kept Yani`s arms stretched out. "Stand up," Jem ordered, then walked out into the passage, still pulling on the rope. Yani stumbled forwards after him, his arm stretched out, and Cob laughed.

"Get used to it. This is how we`re to take you to the pit. Keep your right arm in front and follow Jem. I`ll haul your left arm back so`s you can`t cause any trouble."

Down into the mountain they went, Yani straining to keep his elbows bent and so save his shoulders. Eventually the passage widened and they came to an iron gate. Jem opened it and went in. Beyond lay a circular arena surrounded by walls about six metres tall. A bright light focussed on the sandy floor, ominously stained in several places. The area above brooded in darkness. Jem fastened his rope to a ring on the wall and tossed a key onto the floor.

166

"That`ll get your cuffs off," he said. "There`s a long triton in the corner you`ll need. Don`t want to make it too easy for Hector." He spat on the floor and turned away. "Come on Cob, get out of here," and they left, locking the gate behind them.

Yani grabbed the key and unlocked his iron cuffs. Who was Hector? A dangerous fellow no doubt, but "I know something about fighting now," Yani told himself as he picked up the triton. What else did he have? He looked down at his heavy cuffs lying on the floor but still tied to the two bits of ropes.

A deep voice came from above. "I think you`ll have some difficulty escaping Hector`s embrace. You`ve annoyed me long enough. Still, if your mother will agree to my demands I will order Swarth here to use his stun gun on Hector and you may live a collared life serving me."

Yani looked up into the dark. Ignoring Krask he called, "Mother, are you there?"

An anguished sob came down, "Yani, I`m here."

Krask leant across and spoke softly, each word dripping with malice. "I will have my way. I don`t believe you can sit there and watch your only son torn to bits by Hector when a word from you would save him. Give me your promise to marry me and give me a child. I know an Ell promise is unbreakable."

Elaire, tied to her chair, lifted her chin and spoke in an imperious voice. "Yes it is, but you know little of Ells if you imagine I would ever give you a child. You would corrupt its very soul. How could Yani live, knowing the price paid for his life?"

Krask scoffed." I think you`ll change your mind. The gorrats killed old Zandor, so now there are no Ells left to save you. Soon I shall be the master of this land. You can be my wife, my companion and I`ll give you leave to do your good deeds, and your son shall live."

Her voice rose. "Neither I nor my son will ever bow to your threats, but if you have him killed, I will make you a different promise now—of a vengence beyond your imaginings. Better you release me from this chair and put me down in that pit beside him."

Krask shrugged off her threat and gave a signal. The tunnel gate opened. Yani moved towards it, weight on his toes and every sense alert. A familiar grunting sounded and his spirits sank; so Hector was a gorrat!

The huge shape shambled forward into the pit, blinking against the light. A terrified gasp came from Elaire. Hector, largest of all the gorrats, finally noticed Yani. He opened his jaws and moved forwards eagerly, with great clawed hands reaching for his prey.

Yani jumped sideways and started to swing his ropes, the iron cuffs at the end gathering momentum. Hector changed direction and again Yani leapt sideways. Now he had speed on the ropes. Judging it carefully, he swung the iron cuffs at maximum velocity to smash into Hector's left elbow.

The gorrat's scream split the air. It staggered backwards, clutching its useless left arm, then blinded by fury it charged forwards. Again Yani's speed saved him and he had the rope swinging once more. A blow to Hector's head had no effect however and Yani moved back to gain some space. As long as he could keep dancing round the creature in a circle he could stay alive, but its strength would outlast his. He had to strike it again and break the other arm.

Wary of the swinging missile Hector kept his right arm in and Yani had only the hand to aim at—a much smaller target. On his third attempt he connected and heard the wrist break.

Now the gorrat's most dangerous weapons were disabled. Bemused, Hector shook his head, this had never happened before.

Yani snatched up the triton and went on the offensive. Prodding at Hector's chest he tried to drive him back. Roaring defiance, Hector kept leaping towards Yani so that his terrible jaws could do their work. Every time he sprang forwards Yani skipped sideways and stabbed the triton into Hector's side.

Slowly the constant pain wore down the gorrat's resistance, and it started to back away. Little by little Yani drove Hector

168

back, jabbing with the triton. Yani guessed he would have only one lunge to kill the creature. If he missed his target and the triton ended stuck in Hector's side, Yani would have lost his only weapon. The swinging cuffs could cow, but not kill.

Backed against the wall, Hector snarled and snapped. Yani gripped the triton firmly, readied himself and lunged with all his weight behind the thrust. Hector gasped, his head went back, his legs gave way and he toppled forward, tearing the triton from Yani's hands. Heart hammering, Yani jumped backwards, ready to retreat further, but the great mound of fur didn't move; Hector was dead. A silence fell and Yani stared up into the darkness.

At last Krask found his voice. "Very clever, boy," he sneered. "Are you quite sure you wouldn't like to join my army—I could offer you a fine position."

"Why don't you give up your mad campaign, there's no way you can win."

"Reject my offer? You're as stubborn as your mother. Well let's see how you do against two gorrats. This time you will die."

Yani clenched his jaw. He realized that Krask would not let him live. He lifted his head, "Bring them on," he said and picked up his cuffs again.

2

Peter's Quest

Peter ate some of the food then fell asleep. It was strange being in his old home, strange and very empty. Pasco had told him to stay inside till he got back, but it was now morning and no one had come. Also there was no sign of Yani—something was wrong. Well, he knew his way around and could look after himself. Peter left the house and climbed up to the rocks. Reaching the entrance he was astonished to see Yani's staff lying there abandoned.

"Yani?" he called.

Getting no reply, Peter picked up the staff and immediately it shone a light down into the tunnel. "Yani needs help," he decided and, gripping the staff tightly, set off down into the mountain. After a time he came to the lit passageway and saw a number of doors. Peter moved very slowly, checking each one. One was locked and, peering through the grill, Peter saw a number of guards fast asleep.

Peter left them and went on. Coming to a cell that stood open he looked inside. Apart from iron rings set in the walls, it was quite empty. He trotted down the corridor for some time till it widened. In the distance he spotted three figures walking in a line. Peter recognized Yani in the middle.

They stopped at an iron gate, opened it and went in. Two minutes later the two men came back out without Yani. In a moment they would see him and Peter looked for somewhere to hide. There was an opening in the wall on his right. He darted in and found a small round space with a ladder leading up into darkness. "I'd be safer up there," he thought, and quickly climbed up onto a dimly lit platform. He looked up to see where the light was coming from and saw another opening higher up. A second ladder awaited, but he had no sooner set foot on it than he heard voices coming from below. The men had returned and for some reason were starting to climb the ladder.

"We'll get a view from the top, Cob," a voice floated up.

"You go first, Jem," the other said.

"I'll be trapped," Peter thought then, noticing the ladder top was tied to a bar, he undid the rope and pushed the ladder sideways.

A yell came from below as Jem lost his grip and slipped back onto Cob, kicking him in the face. Cob fell all the way to the ground but Jem managed to cling on until he got his feet back on the rungs. Carefully he climbed down to see to Cob, who lay moaning on the floor.

"I told you to secure that thing properly, you idiot," he shouted. "Hector will be passing shortly and he could smell us in here. We've got to get up that ladder."

Cob didn't move so Jem said, "Suit yourself," and started back up, this time holding on tightly. Peter stepped back into the shadow and gripped the staff. Hands appeared, then the dark shape of Jem's head filled the opening. Peter swung the staff down as hard as he could. There was a sickening thud and Jem disappeared. Peter heard the body hit the ground.

Now there was silence; even Cob had stopped moaning. Peter peered down and made out two motionless figures. Neither seemed to be conscious. Using all his strength he managed to haul the ladder up, thus securing his position. He sat down to recover. Some time later he heard other sounds coming from above. He turned to the second ladder and climbed up onto a small balcony overlooking the arena. An angry voice was saying something about two gorrats. Looking down, Peter saw Yani standing in the middle of the floor. Against the wall lay a huge hairy shape, with a triton stuck in its chest, obviously quite dead.

Straight across from him was a viewing gallery, dimly lit. A large bearded man was pointing his hand down towards Yani and saying, "This time you will die."

Peter took a deep breath. "Yani," he called. "Catch," and threw down the staff. It landed at Yani's feet. Yani stared at the familiar object lying before him, then looked up.

"Peter?" he said, unbelievingly.

"It's your staff. Pick it up!"

Hope waking, Yani seized the staff, shouted "Up!" and jumped.

Krask gaped at Yani, who had just leapt six metres from the floor and now stood on the gallery, both hands on his staff. Elaire, collar linked to her chair, sat on Krask's left. Beyond, her guard raised his stun gun and fired but Elaire's arm shot out, hitting the gun and spoiling his aim. The charge only grazed Yani's hand, but it knocked his staff across the floor.

Recovering himself, Krask stood up. He smiled like a hungry wolf. "I'll just need to deal with you myself, boy," He put his hand in a side pocket and held out a key. "This is what you want, isn't it? Come and get it."

His staff was hidden somewhere in the gloom behind. Yani knew Krask wouldn't give him leeway to look for it. A yell came from the guard behind as Elaire grabbed his arm and broke it. The gun fell out of his hand and over the balcony.

Krask looked round, and at that moment Yani threw himself forward in a rolling somersault dive, then, his back on the floor, kicked upwards into the massive belly. Krask, all breath driven out, staggered back. His hands opened and the precious key fell into Yani's swift hand.

Rolling sideways Yani sprang to his feet. He kicked hard at the guard's knee and, as the fellow crumpled, Yani dropped the key into Elaire's lap. "Yani, behind you," she shouted, and he swung round.

One hand clutched to his stomach, the other reaching out, the huge figure lurched forward. Yani grabbed Krask's hand, pulling it forwards as he fell onto his back and again kicked up into Krask's stomach. Unable to stop, his body lifted by Yani's legs, Krask crashed headfirst over the railing and down into the pit. Suddenly, all was still.

Yani turned to Elaire who had just unlocked her collar and, beyond speech, wrapped her in his arms for a brief moment of relief. Shadows of an agonizing fear drained from her face and she took his face between trembling hands. Her eyes drank in the bruised, exhausted face of this boy, this young man, her son, who had fought to save them.

"Yani, my boy my boy," she sobbed, "oh my son, you've beaten them and set us free." Her voice grew stronger, "Now to stay free. Is that monster dead?"

Yani looked over the balcony and saw Krask twitching on the ground.

"Not yet, I'd better get my staff." He looked at the guard.

"Don't worry about him," Elaire said. "I surprised him with the strength of an Ell."

She laid a hand on the guard's head and he became unconscious. "He won't waken for hours," she said.

Yani remembered something. "Mother, Peter is on that balcony. I must get him down. Also Grandpa and the others will still be looking for the main entrance."

A tremendous crash startled them and they looked down. The iron gate into the arena had burst open and three figures stood there. Zandor, Arlinda and Ragore had arrived. They gazed at the scene in amazement. Yani`s laughter rang out, an alien sound in that place of death.

"You`ve found the back way in. Well, there`s a prisoner for you lying on the floor. Stay there, I`m coming down."

All three heads stared up into the gloom as Yani`s voice was recognized.

Elaire, wanting to surprise her parents, spoke quietly to Yani. "There`s a stair down to the pit. Let`s join them."

The three in the arena were staring at the moaning hulk of Krask, when an unexpected small voice from above said, "Is it safe to come down now?"

Zandor swung round. "Peter? Peter, where are you?"

"I`m stuck on this balcony and there are two nasty men at the foot of the ladder. I think they`ll want to kill me."

Ragore was already running back. "I`ll fix them," he growled. "Hold on a moment." He found the entrance off the corridor and two confused men stumbling to their feet.

"Back against the wall," Ragore snapped, "and don`t move."

Neither Cob nor Jem took advice easily. Ragore`s staff blasted Cob against the wall and his fist knocked Jem senseless. "That felt good," he said, rubbing his hand. He stared up as Peter lowered the ladder. "Come down now, little fellow. These two are sleeping again."

Wide-eyed, Peter viewed his pursuers. "Let`s tie them up," he suggested. "They were nasty to Yani." He knelt and, with some help from Ragore, moved Jem behind Cob. He tied a rope round Cob`s neck with the other end around Jem`s wrists. He then did the same exercise in reverse, sat back and grinned.

"Perhaps they`ll manage to strangle each other," he said.

Ragore stifled a laugh. "Wherever did you learn that? Anyway they're safe enough for now," he said. "Let's join the others."

Re-entering the arena, they found Zandor and Arlinda weeping with their arms around a tall lady, who seemed equally moved. Yani stood alone, keeping his staff pointed at Krask, who had only been winded by the fall.

Peter, oblivious of the reunion, shouted, "He did it, he did it, without his staff. He killed Hector."

At last the impact of what the boy was saying got through to Zandor. He looked at his grandson. "What is he saying, Yani? What did you do?"

"It's true, Father," Elaire said. "I've a most resourceful son," and she started to explain.

Yani, embarrassed, stopped her. "Later, Mother, later. We need to get this place cleared out. Grandpa's asked for guards from Madrid but we need to open the main entrance for them."

"I've had many tours of Krask's domain, when he was trying to impress me with his budding empire. I can show you where everything is. We should go to the central ampitheatre and send for all his commanders. You will summon them for me, won't you, Krask?" The gentle voice held shards of steel.

An hour later the Ells stood on the dais facing a motly assembly of bewildered people. Elaire separated the commanders and stood them to one side. "You know who I am, but you have never met me uncollared, so beware! I know many of you have also been prisoners, and for you rescue is on the way. For the rest, guards are flying up from Madrid and you will be sent for rehabilitation. Fail that, and you will spend the rest of your days working to survive on a lonely island."

She turned to Krask. "You are too great a danger to remain alive here, especially after we three leave earth."

Yani interrupted her. "I have an idea, Mother," and he spoke quietly to her for a minute.

Elaire, shocked, turned on Zandor. "You put another man's memory into my son's head. How could you? He's only fourteen."

It was I," Arlinda said, "at the direct instructions of the Elders. Remember he'd already been to the Tower, so sixteen is a better gauge. "

Elaire looked from one to the other. "Yani wants to give Krask the same implant, to show him how wrong he has been."

Zandor grunted, "It'll probably send him mad. However he is a man of great strength and ability, well worth saving if we can."

"We should try. We don't know where his daughters have gone and any chance of persuading him to help us should be taken." Arlinda spoke with conviction. "It's a splendid idea, Yani."

"Swarth, the gorrat handler is also missing," Elaire said. "Perhaps he's gone with the daughters."

"We'll need to destroy all these creatures. Do you know where they are kept?" Yani asked her. Before she could answer, Swarth, who had been busy assembling the gorrats, launched his counter-attack. Hordes of the creatures poured out of a side tunnel grunting ferociously, fangs shining and claws hungry for their victims.

"Freeze them," Yani shouted and the Rainbow staffs shone bright yellow beams on the advancing creatures. They slowed, turned white and stopped, killed instantly by intense cold. Swarth, egging them on, suffered the same fate. A few of the little ones at the back panicked and, unseen, turned and ran away.

During this interruption, Elaire kept her eyes on Krask and his commanders, none of whom dared to move.

Ragore drew a shaky breath. "Well that saves us looking for them in those endless tunnels. What do we do now?"

"Get the main gate open then bring in Martinelli and his guards," Zandor said. "You'll be pleased to know that Turias is back from America and will be coming with them.

CHAPTER EIGHTEEN

1

Ellshome

Three days later Martinelli`s flyer landed at the lakeside buildings and the officer hurried inside.

"Just in time for lunch, Captain," Ragore called. "We`re eating the last of our supplies—no point in wasting them."

Martinelli looked at Zandor. "The situation is under control now. All Krask`s people have been dispersed and I have two hundred guards collecting all his weapons and stores. No more of these awful creatures have been found, but my men still carry powerful stun guns just in case. Krask himself has been sent to Altania as you wished."

"And there`s still no sign of his daughters?" Yani asked, only to receive an exasperated look from Turias.

"Yani, you must try and forget her."

"I know, but we must try to find them. Zenia at least still harbours dangerous ideas. Captain, if you find any information let us know at once, please."

Martinelli smiled, "Of course."

"We shall fly to Madrid and collect our friends from the hospital this afternoon," Zandor said, "after returning our young hero here to Marmorian. I hope to do that before Janine finds out what we`ve put him through. Also, I need you to return our horses to Taca and my Kuzak to Marmorian. Salvador agreed he could spend the rest of the winter there."

Martinelli nodded, then looked at Peter, busy attacking the lunch Ragore had put in front of him. "Have you ever thought of joining the guards, young fellow?"

Peter`s face lit up. "Aren`t I a bit small?"

"If you continue eating like that, you`ll grow soon enough," Yani laughed. "I think the Captain meant when you`re grown up."

Peter scowled, "That`ll take years," he said.

"Time for you to think about it," Zandor said.

Arriving in Madrid they were relieved to find Lucy fully recovered. "Now we can all return to Altania," Zandor said, "but on the way there is one more thing to do."

Despite questions, he would say no more, so Pasco and Lucy spent the flight getting every detail of Yani`s adventures out of him.

"That`s the second time little Peter`s saved you, Yani. He`s become a real talisman," Pasco remarked.

"It`s quite strange, isn`t it?" his sister added, "but he`ll find life a little dull now, back with Janine."

Yani nodded. "If he hadn`t brought my staff—"

Elaire turned round and said, "Please don`t even think about it."

As Zandor landed the flyer Yani looked out, surprised. "I know where we are," he said, "it`s below that strange hill with the stones I passed before I met you."

"Yes," his grandfather said, "the Hill of Farewell. Now we are all going somewhere entirely different. Bring your staffs." He climbed out and led the way up the bare hillside. A bitter wind blew from the north but the climb, and the expectation of something new, warmed the youngsters.

"Let us older ones catch our breath, then I`ll explain." Zandor said.

Elaire offered. "I can do so, Father." She looked at the eager faces and smiled.

"This is a Place of Power, a Portal, where those with Ell genes can cross over into another dimension and reach our world. To get there the first time you must prepare your minds as if for meditating, the second time is easier. Take deep breaths and relax. Think of finding a place of true sanctuary."

She waited while the group relaxed. "Now," she said quietly, "drive your staffs into the ground, and think 'Home.'"

"Home," they thought. All light vanished. The ground disappeared under their feet, and they fell into dazzling fountains of colours before finding they could stand again. Beyond the swirl of colours, a landscape beckoned.

"Walk forward," Elaire said. They stepped out from the fountain onto springy turf. Before them stretched parklands studded with great trees. A feeling of great peace permeated the very air and there seemed to be a gentle music coming from far away. Stupified, the youngsters gazed around. Yani found his voice first. "Where are our staffs?"

"Guarding our space on Earth, against our return."

"It`s like a summer`s evening in the far north," Lucy said. "Look, there are stars appearing, but they don`t look familiar."

"They wouldn`t," Zandor said. "We are a long way from Earth."

"What is that hill up ahead with the line of pillars—it reminds me of the Temple at the Tower?" Yani asked.

"That`s where we`re going," his mother replied, leading the way over the grass.

At the hill`s foot they found a wide marble staircase and started to climb. Up and up they went discovering that after each flight of twenty one steps there was a landing that allowed them to draw breath. At the beginning of each new set of stairs a door was set at the side.

"These doors don`t lead to a lift, by any chance?" Ragore asked hopefully.

"No, they open onto a corridor that leads to halls under the hill, but no lift, Ragore. You just have to climb."

"These steps are easy," Lucy said. "I feel so well here, I want to run up them."

Still they climbed and the pillars appeared to grow in size. They curved away into a misty distance both on the right and on the left. Finally the group reached the top.

A gigantic piazza, paved with pale rose coloured stone, opened before them. Far off in the middle, as if it had grown there, stood a hexagonal cathedral, built of the same stone. Each of the eight faces presented an archway, shimmering with colours, and, from the point of each arch, the roofline soared up to a central, golden spire.

"It`s like a jewel, the most exquisite jewel," breathed Lucy.

Distant music hung in the sweet evening air, lending enchantment to the scene. Yani started to move towards the cathedral but Elaire laid a gentle hand on his shoulder. "Not yet, my son. Not for a very long time. That's where we go at our ending."

Turias had so far not uttered a word, but the eyes in the usually impassive face were alive with interest. Suddenly, "Who is that waving at us?" he asked, pointing to a tall figure striding towards them.

"That will be a member of our Council coming to arrange the time when Zandor, Elaire and I are to leave Earth." Arlinda replied.

"What, so soon?" Yani cried in alarm, and was joined by more protests from his friends. "I've just found Mother and my family, and you are going to leave?"

Sadness filled Zandor's eyes. "Believe me Yani, we do not wish to go, but all pure Ells must depart. Our work on Earth is done and we've already stretched out our time to find your Mother. I doubt that even Zelton can give us much more leeway."

"Zelton? But he was the one who started the Intervention— and he's still alive?"

"Still alive?" a deep voice laughed, "I sincerely hope so. Here we hardly age at all. So you are Yani. I've heard much about you. Yes, I am Zelton and I have no wish to break up your family immediately, but the Council have set a deadline."

Yani stared back at this commanding presence, who had approached so quickly. He spoke from his heart. "I must surely be allowed time to get to know my Mother."

"The special circumstances have been taken into account and the Council have agreed an extension until a year in the coming autumn. However Zandor, Arlinda and Elaire must start to delegate as much as possible to you young Guardians."

"Only a year and a half—"

"Quiet, Yani," Elaire said. "That is most considerate, Zelton. Please thank the Council on our behalf. I need to explain more to these young people."

"Indeed," Zelton said, "now Zandor and Arlinda can tell me more about events on Earth while you do so. We three shall stroll for a while," and with one arm on Zandor`s shoulder and the other on Arlinda`s, he led them off.

"I`ve good news for all of you," Elaire said, smiling at Pasco, Lucy, Ragore and Turias. "Your mothers all returned here from Earth and you may come and visit them from time to time."

"Mother here?" Lucy cried. "Oh Pasco, I can`t believe it. When can we meet?"

"Beyond that pillar behind us, you`ll find the Hall of Exile. They are waiting there to welcome you. Yani and I will join you later."

The four students rushed off and Elaire said, "You see Yani, that even after we leave Earth, you will be able to visit me here from time to time. Later, when your work on Earth is finished, we will be waiting for you. Now come and see something else."

"That`s wonderful," Yani said, "so I won`t lose you forever—. "

His voice broke off as they walked past the next pillar. "That`s impossible," he cried, gazing at a huge range of snow covered mountains.

"No, Yani. You see each gap looks down onto a different world. Walk past the next pillar." Fifty paces on, Yani gasped again. Before him stretched a grey ocean, where winds whipped foam from the wave tops and clouds hurried across a darkening sky.

"Walk down any of these steps and you will find gateways to these worlds."

"How many different gateways are there?"

"We don`t know, we have never found an end to this promenade. It is called the Last Corniche and the further it goes, the stranger the worlds become."

"But surely this hill is round?"

Elaire shrugged, "It only seems so. I suspect it`s a spiral. From here we can explore forever. Indeed there is an ancient legend that the Arraqail went that way long ago, before disappearing from the physical worlds altogether. Perhaps they now exist on a higher plane.

"Now you have seen the heritage of the Ells, I can show you no more. You and your friends have much of what you need to begin your task on Earth, so tonight, in the Hall of Exile, we shall have a splendid party to celebrate the launch of the Guardians."

"Then we have to return to Earth and –"

"Then after further studies, your real work will begin."

Yani nodded then said, "I would like to walk along this great promenade for a little while on my own."

Elaire frowned. "Don`t go too far, remember what I told you."

Though unsure why he had this sudden compulsion, Yani began to walk along the mysterious way. He had the impression something was waiting for him, but whether it was friendly or not, he had no idea. After passing many of the great pillars, visibility diminished. Mist closed round him and gradually all feeling left his body.

"Am I still walking?" he asked out loud, and an answer rang in his mind.

"That is of no consequence, Rainbow Jewel carrier. As Ellshome is on a higher level than Earth so we now are on a higher octave again and have no more contact with dense material.

"We are the Arraqail and it is our Staff and Jewel that you bear. So far you have found four companions. There are seven colours so you must find three more to carry the remaining staves, which are still embedded in your staff. Thus will the Rainbow Warriors be founded. All will be needed, for there is a great and terrible enemy awaiting the time when you young Guardians stand alone. In time you will need the white staff, which is in the keeping of Alicia. She lives in a convent in the Hebrides and has great spiritual powers. Listen to what she has to tell you, especially about meditation.

"Now, hold out your hand." Yani did so, and felt a ring being slipped onto his little finger. "This is the Jewel`s Ring of Finding. You will be able to find anyone who wears it, no matter where they are. Use it wisely. Now return to your people."

Almost reluctantly, Yani turned and started to retrace his steps. As he went the mist gradually dispersed and sensation returned to his legs. In the distance Elaire stood waiting. When he reached her, she looked searchingly into his eyes but said nothing. Laying her hand on his shoulder she turned and led him off to the Hall of Exile, where music, laughter and friends were waiting.

* * * * *

Epilogue

1

Polonia. 1st March 2437

Leaving their flyer hidden among some trees, two cloaked and hooded figures walked down the hill into Polonia. Reaching Senga`s cottage they stopped and knocked on the door. There was the sound of a bolt being drawn then the door swung open. Cane in hand, Senga stepped out, her eyes inspecting the figures suspiciously. Both of them carried strong looking staffs.

"Good afternoon," she said, "can I help you?"

The smaller of the two threw back his hood, and there was the distinctive blaze of golden hair she had known so well. Older, more mature, but still unmistakable, Yani`s face grinned at her, the blue eyes sparkling with mischief. "Hullo, Senga," he said, "have you baked my birthday cake?"

She swayed and shot out her hand to grasp the doorpost.

"Yani?" she gasped, "is it really you?"

"Of course, and this is Turias, my friend."

Senga glanced around hurriedly, then said "Come inside, quickly."

Once they had entered, she closed and bolted the door behind them.

"Did anyone see you come down the hill?"

"I don`t think so. Why would it matter?" Turias asked

Senga looked up at this young giant and said, "It`s good you`re so big. Jord has assembled a large number of outlaws. Apparently something important happened up north and the man who had been buying stuff from them has disappeared. They`ve had no money for months now, so Jord has gathered them together into a force that will be able to attack small towns. He will have enough men now to seize you, even if half of what was said about your escape is true. Hide here and after dark—."

Yani smiled. "I'm pleased he's here and it sounds as if he's saved us a lot of trouble.

We've come to capture him and any other outlaws that can be found."

Senga frowned. "Yani, don't get carried away. That's nonsense, but sit down and tell me what has happened to you. In one year you seem to have grown three at least."

Yani glanced at Turias, smiled and said, "Well, we've plenty of time," and launched into a brief tale of his travels. His explanation of the powers of the Ells astonished Senga. "I thought they had all gone," she said, "though I knew there was something special about you, I never guessed it was anything to do with the Ells."

A thunderous banging on the door startled her.

"Hide," she whispered, "I have a cellar and—."

"Senga," Yani said, "there is nothing to worry about. We've dealt with much worse things than outlaws." He turned to Turias and nodded.

They both pulled up their hoods and Turias slipped back the bolt and, flinging the door open, strode out so rapidly that the two men outside staggered backwards.

"Why are you making so much noise?" Turias demanded.

Somewhat intimidated by the size of this fellow, the older of the two fought to restore his dignity. He drew himself up to his full height and announced, "All visitors to Polonia must report to Captain Jord."

"Ridiculous," snapped Turias. "Never heard of him. We are travelling monks and bring peace wherever we go. We are our own masters."

Yani's voice from behind said, "Perhaps, Brother T, we should comply with local custom and allow this good fellow to lead us to this Captain. What is your name, by the way?"

Soothed by the gentler tone, the man said his name was Letta and his companion Veld.

"Well Letta, take us to Captain Jord."

Worried and mystified by Yani's behaviour, Senga followed the men as they led the way right through the village and back to Jord's farm at the far end. Yani thought little had changed till they reached the farm but then, behind it, he saw a large group of tents.

"Siesta time," Letta commented, "but you'll find the Captain awake and working in his house."

"Thank you," Yani said, "Now it's time for your siesta," and he laid his staff gently on Letta's head. There was a humming noise and Letta collapsed.

"Now Veld, I suggest you run and tell the Captain that there are a couple of mad, dangerous monks who wish to speak with him."

Veld stared at the two figures as he backed away, then spun round and ran off towards the house as fast as his legs could carry him.

"I think we should deepen the siesta," Turias suggested. "I'll attend to it." He pointed his staff towards the tents and a shimmering bubble formed over them.

"Here comes Jord," Yani murmured, and Turias turned to see an angry looking man striding towards them. He was followed by a dozen others, all of them armed with various weapons. Jord was shouting.

"What are you doing in my village? Strangers are not welcome here, unless," and he looked at Turias, "they wish to join my band. You look a useful size."

"I am not a stranger, Jord, I grew up here," and Yani flung back his hood and stepped forward.

Jord gaped at him in disbelief. "Yani the brat! You've come back—now I can deal with you." He leapt forwards, but Turias grabbed him behind the neck with a grip that made him yelp, then forced him to his knees.

"Not so fast, Captain."

"Help me," Jord croaked to the men behind. They started forwards, only to be halted by another bubble, spun out of Yani's staff. Imprisoned, the men threw themselves against the thin but unyielding wall, in an effort to obey Jord.

"We have not come to join your band, Jord. We've come to destroy it." Jord fought to free himself from Turias's grip. His eyes bulged with the effort and his face flamed with temper. "I should have thrashed you harder," he spluttered. "You and that old man I allowed to stay here."

"Allowed, Jord? This was his home, a happy village till you terrorized it. Well that`s all over. You and your band of thugs are going to re-habillitation, though I expect it may be rather late for you. I expect you`ll spend the rest of your life working with the desert reclamation squads. Where is that dreadful son of yours?"

Jord glared at him and spat. Just at that moment, their curiosity aroused by Jord`s shout, three figures emerged from the house. Yani subdued a surge of anger as Marc, Lula and Venty approached. Noticing the men struggling inside a huge bubble, and seeing that Jord was helpless in the grip of a huge, forbidding black-cloaked figure, they halted some metres off and stared at Yani.

"I told you he was a witch," whispered Lula.

"No witch, but an Ell—as you nicknamed me," Yani said softly. "I`ve come to remove you all, and see you get a decent education before it`s too late. Thugs raise thugs and you need a better chance."

Marc and Venty, allowed to run wild all their lives, looked around for assistance.

"Your army is sleeping deeply in that big bubble," Turias told them. "These ruffians are held in that smaller one and I have your leader under control. Now shall I bubble you too, or will you remain still? I suggest you sit down."

The three looked at each other, then slowly sank down. Yani stared at them and felt his long held anger melt away. They really were poor misguided creatures, perhaps re-hab could help them. He took a V-phone out of his pocket and spoke into it.

A few minutes later six large flyers flew in and landed nearby. The distinctive, smart figure of Captain Martinelli was first out. "You`ve had no trouble Yani?" he asked. "We`ve only been on standby for an hour or so."

187

"No trouble, but we've caught more fish than expected. This rascal," and Yani indicated Jord now kneeling motionless in Turias's unrelenting grip, "has assembled most of the remaining outlaws for us. They are sleeping in these tents over there. There must be about a hundred of them. That'll save you a deal of hunting for them."

Martinelli was delighted. "I'll need some further transport from Madrid," he said. "It'll take a few hours to organize, so meanwhile we will handcuff the sleepers."

"Let me lift the bubble, we don't want your men to join the deep sleepers," Turias grinned. "But I suggest these three young ones here are taken first. Yani can send that dozen to sleep before he lifts the small bubble."

"I would like to return to my old friend Senga," Yani said. "We were rudely interrupted and I know she wants to hear more."

Martinelli turned to his men and issued a series of orders, then he turned to Yani and Turias, and shook their hands with great vigour.

"I can take it from here. Thank you both for your help, it's saved us a great deal of time hunting through the country for these rascals."

Leaving the flabbergasted Jord, Marc, Lula and Venty in Martinelli's hands Yani and Turias escorted Senga back to her home. She kept glancing at Yani as if reassuring herself that this was really the young lad who had left Polonia just a year ago.

Later, after she had heard the rest of his story, she gave a great sigh and, with the worries of years falling from her shoulders, stood up, took Yani's face in her hands and said, "Yani, you have brought relief to a village that gave you nothing but sorrow. Now you can return to your own folk with a clear mind, and with my fondest blessing. I am so pleased that you found your mother, give her my best wishes."

"You can do that yourself, Senga. She intends to visit you next month to thank you for what you did for me. I shall come with her as well to see that the new arrangements are going well. Now Turias and I must return to Altania to complete our training, it seems there is always more to learn. But before we leave tell me what you knew of the Ells and what they did."

Senga scratched her head. "Not much," she replied. " My parents died early and my grandmother brought me here. She was the village healer and even then Pollonia had no connection with the Ell culture. She did tell me that the Ell schools told the story of the Great Island. In another place and time there was a huge island in the middle of which rose the highest mountain in all the world. From this mountain four rivers ran, north, east, south and west. Each carved wide valleys with steep sides so that the people who lived there were quite cut off from contact with any other valley.

"Each had quite a different view of the mountain's shining peak, a sight so beautiful that all the islanders believed that this was God's dwelling. To the people in the north the peak shone white, but from the eastern valley it glowed at dawn and this became the time for their worship. For those in the south the peak was brightest at noon and for the western dwellers the golden hues at evening, shining even when the shore was dark, became the holy time.

"Apparently the Ells used this fable to demonstrate the divisions that separated humankind. There was only one mountain though it could be viewed from many different places. Many of the religions on Earth tended to be exclusive—only their beliefs were right and everyone else was wrong. A peaceful civilisation demanded a base of tolerance, this is what they taught."

Yani nodded. "Yes, I was told this tale too and Turias of course learned it when he started school. Now Senga we must go, but I shall visit you again."

The old healer smiled. "I must see this flying thing of yours and make syre you leave without any further excitements."

She walked up the hill with them, determined to see their amazing flying machine. It would make a fitting end to this day of miracles.

FAREWELL.

10th October 2438

Extract from Zandor`s final address to the World Council.

Your Excellencies, I am here today to wish you farewell. It is over four centuries since the Intervention and now we Ells must allow humankind to resume full control of their destiny.

When we came this world was in a parlous state with a population that was rapidly outgrowing the planet`s resources. Conflicts were growing and economic and political systems coming under ever increasing pressures. Most of Earth`s people did not enjoy individual freedom. Conflicting beliefs were fired up by leaders intent on acquiring power. Gathering weapons containing powerful destructive technology they presented a real threat to peace.

From today`s viewpoint it is easier to grasp this general picture but at the time of our arrival there was no general welcome given to our advice. As gently as possible, though not without opposition, we imposed our solutions steadily over time. Now we leave a planet at peace, with stable world wide government based upon individual freedom.

We leave only a small group of Guardians, all of them half Ell and half human, who have been trained to deal with any untoward activities arising from the misuse of purloined Ell technology. They are your servants and can only be dismissed by a majority vote of the full Council, all fifty seven of you.

While we believe that Earth`s civilization is now soundly established, there remain remote communities where Ell schools and influence have not been accepted. We have seldom sought to impose our will, preferring to lead by example and it is now in your hands how to extend our teachings of tolerance and peace.

Much of our technology has been absorbed, and your universities are full of students keen to develop new ideas and encourage the further evolution of humankind.

191

I, and the few of my colleagues who are left, will depart Earth in a few day`s time. We will pray for your success but we shall not return.

I wish you a wonderful future. Farewell.

The following is an extract from the second volume of Legends of the Ells, entitled "The Young Guardians" to be published next year.

The Terror Wave

A shaft of red light shone down upon the Pacific island like a celestial knife. Its white hot heat pierced the rock on the mountainside, burrowing a deep chasm. Steadily it moved northwards carving the mountain in two. Finally, with an awesome roar, half of the towering rock face fell into the sea. The resulting gigantic tsunami would now pulse eastwards through the ocean for thousands of miles before wrecking its fury on whatever land it reached.

The Peruvian Coast. 19th October 2438

Kathryn walked by the ocean, her dark green eyes mournful as she remembered Fiella, her Ell mother.

"Why must you go?" she had asked Fiella, six months before. "Isn`t life here good enough for you? Look how unhappy Dad is!"

Fiella`s eyes swam and she bit her lip. "Believe me, my darling, if I could stay I would, but you know that all Ells must leave this planet. Perhaps I should never have married Dad but we have been so happy all these years—and we wouldn`t have had you, the joy of our life. You know that you can come with me to Ellshome—"

"And leave Dad alone? I couldn`t, you know that. I love you both." Kathryn buried her face in her hands and sobbed. "It seems so unfair."

Fiella cradled the blonde head in her arms.

"Life brings sorrow as well as joy. Dad knew this day would come, I knew it too, but the Ells have been here for centuries and we had hoped for a longer time together. However the Council have decreed that now humankind should show they can manage unaided, so we must go. Only the half-Ells can

193

choose to stay….. my darling, this is like dying for me too…"
Fiella's voice broke and Kathryn wrapped her arms around her
mother's shoulders.

"A true child of nature," murmured Fiella to her husband
Alain, on their last night together. "She will be a comfort to
you when I'm gone. It's so hard this parting, though we
always knew it would come some day. If only I could take you
with me!" Her husband's lip quivered as he stroked her hair.
"No, my dearest love," he whispered, "we married with our
eyes open and I wouldn't change a thing. If you stayed longer
you would see me age before your eyes, then die and leave
you alone. This is cleaner and better. You have given this
world a great gift in Kathryn. Soon she will go to the
Guardians, all of whom have vanished Ell mothers, and learn
to preserve the Ell legacy. Kathryn is our gift to the world."
    Following her mother's departure, the bond between
Kathryn and Alain deepened. Now she was sixteen she would
travel to Altania, where she would study to become a
Guardian, and Alain would be totally alone. The night before
he left for his annual visit to Juliaca, high up in the Andes, he
had a talk with her about the future.
    "You are ready to do all that your Mother and I could wish
for—join the other students and use your talents to guard the
legacy of the Ells. Someone will collect you tomorrow
evening and bring you up to Juliaca before you go on to
Altania. I don't own you, darling, and I must try to make a
new life for myself—but we shall meet often. At least you are
staying on Earth."
    After Alain had left early in the morning, Kathryn decided
to walk along the shore to a distant cave she had heard of. This
would be her last chance to investigate it before leaving her
old home. She sang as she walked, an old Paraguyan song of
farewell, her young voice winging out on the morning air.
    Walking helped her think and calmed her mind. As she
went along, she thought about her forthcoming trip to Altania
and wondered if the Atlantic was as splendid an ocean as this

great Pacific, which she loved as an old friend. She read its moods like a book, and rejoiced in all its various changes.

Today, however, it seemed strange. The sea and the sullen look of the cloudy weather puzzled her; this was a face the Pacific had never shown her, and it did not seem friendly.

"It'll soon cheer up!" she said to herself

Despite the dull weather, Kathryn had left early and consequently was further south than usual. "Dad and I never explored that cave we heard about," she thought. The cliff face stood up clearly now—she would reach it soon. Some distance along it the dark opening of the cave beckoned.

The ocean and sky had turned a strange metallic colour, Kathryn began to feel uncomfortable. Her staff had been trying to attract her attention for some time now but there was no way she could get to a V-phone till she returned home, so she ignored it. Having walked so far, any message could wait.

Still, she could not ignore a growing feeling of apprehension, so she hurried her steps towards her goal. Unbidden, an odd piece of knowledge surfaced in her mind. It was some macabre joke about young men seeking out danger for fun. A sailor, despising their stupidity, had suggested they go down to the beach to watch a tsunami come in.

"A tsunami!" she thought, "no, surely not! There would be a warning", then she looked at her staff and realized her mistake. Panic seized her. The evidence lay before her for the tide had retreated so far it was utterly unnatural. All around had grown deathly quiet. The gulls had fled and there was a growing, frightening anticipation hanging in the air around her; something momentous was coming!

"If it is a tsunami, I'm exposed here. Could the cave protect me?"

Heart pounding, Kathryn began to run, but the sand dragged at her feet and the cave remained agonizingly distant.

Far ahead, where the land ran further out to sea, a dark line appeared. A strange sound vibrated in the air, the ground trembled and the total hopelessness of her situation hit her.

She couldn't reach the cave in time; it probably wouldn't save her anyway.

There was nowhere, simply nowhere she might go and absolutely nothing she could do. She stood on trembling legs staring at her approaching doom. For a mad moment she wondered if anyone had ever tried to surf a tsunami. Her whole body quivered as she grasped her student staff tightly, wishing it had some of the abilities possessed by the fabled staffs of the Guardians. She had been told they could lift you up! She held it out in trembling hands. "Lift me! Lift me!" she commanded it.

Nothing happened. The horizon changed as, far out in front of her, the dark line started to rise.

Lightning Source UK Ltd.
Milton Keynes UK
20 March 2010

151649UK00001B/32/P